SECRET SANTA

WRITTEN BY
Amanda Tru

"Count it all joy, my brothers when you meet trials of various kinds, for you know that the testing of your faith produces steadfastness. And let steadfastness have its full effect, that you may be perfect and complete, lacking in nothing."
James 1:2-4 ESV

CHAPTER 1

It was time for Hailey Rhodes to admit the truth: things were not going well. She was broke, currently dressed as a Christmas elf, and Santa Claus was hitting on her.

Hailey glanced down at her watch. Ugh! Her shift wasn't going to be over for another four hours!

"Am I really that boring, or do you have some place you have to go?" Santa asked, noting her obvious check of the time.

"Neither," Hailey replied, trying to be nice. "I think time would go a lot faster if there were actually kids wanting to see Santa. But the entire store is practically deserted! I didn't understand why we had to start the Santa visits before Thanksgiving anyway. It seems rather pointless to me, but I'm generally opposed to hearing Christmas music right after Halloween too."

"So you're a Scrooge." Santa said, his eyes sparkling with amusement.

"Before Thanksgiving? Definitely, yes. I promise to turn into a merry little elf on Black Friday though."

Santa was quiet, though Hailey felt him studying her out of the corner of his eye. She had to admit, Santa's conversation wasn't pushy or extremely annoying, but by his overly attentive manner, Hailey suspected he was interested in her for more reasons than just to pass a boring shift with a coworker. From watching his body language and the upper part of his face that was visible, he appeared to be a relatively young Santa. And it wasn't as if Hailey already had a boyfriend or even a decent list of prospects. Yet it was difficult to not be put off by the long white beard and plump red suit. If this was God's idea of a Prince Charming for Hailey Rhodes, she really didn't know that she could appreciate His sense of humor.

"How about we make things less boring for you with a friendly little wager?" Santa asked, his eyes flashing a mischievous glint.

"What do you mean?" Hailey asked warily. She was not the gambling sort. But in the last two hours, there had been a total of three children come to visit Santa. Hailey had instead spent the time rearranging every item in the display area and trying to avoid Santa's many attempts to draw her into a conversation. It wasn't that Hailey was unfriendly, but she wasn't a social butterfly. She was already in a bad mood and really couldn't imagine having that much in common with a department store Santa Claus. But at this point, she was getting desperate for almost any distraction. Counting the tiles on the ceiling was beginning to look like a fascinating use of her time. Now if Santa had a better idea . . .

"I think you're wrong about it being a mistake to start the Santa visits so early. I'm willing to bet you that we will have over a hundred kids come to see us before the end of our shift."

"Are you joking?" Hailey asked. "It's the middle of the day. Nobody is going to be coming to see Santa. Parents are at work, and kids are at school. Our shift ends at 6:00. There's nobody in the store right now. I don't see how that is going to change."

Santa shrugged. "Take it or leave it."

"What are the stakes?" Hailey asked. The man didn't appear insane, but if he was foolish enough to make a silly wager, she might just take him up on it.

"If you win and we have less than 100 kids come, then I will give you a $50 gift card to the store."

"And if you win?" Hailey asked.

"You go on a date with me."

Hailey looked at him, really looked at him, for the first time. Was he serious? It was difficult to see much of the man beneath the costume. Hailey knew he was tall, but most men were tall compared to Hailey's petite 5'2'' frame. She couldn't see anything about his physique due to the red suit's heavy padding, and the snowy white beard covered most of his face. The white wig and jolly red hat completely hid his hair. The only features visible were the upper part of his cheeks, his nose, and his eyes. He really didn't appear to be that old. There weren't wrinkles or crows' feet by his eyes. And his clear blue eyes seemed honest and sincere, if not a little roguish. But realistically, would a decent, successful guy around Hailey's age really have a job as a seasonal department store Santa Claus?

Hailey would never consider accepting the wager if money was involved, but a gift card somehow seemed different. If she had that, she might be able to buy her nieces and nephew some nice Christmas presents. There was no way they were going to have over 100 visitors before 5:00, but if

Santa won by some miracle, she could probably handle one date with him. After all, it couldn't be much worse than the other disastrous dates she'd been on in her dating career.

"Okay, you have a deal," Hailey agreed suddenly, almost afraid he'd change his mind. Even if she lost or he didn't follow through on his end of the deal, she would at least appreciate that their little wager had helped pass the time on an extremely boring shift.

Hailey saw Santa's white teeth flash in a smile beneath the beard. "Good!"

"Just what kind of 'date' did you have in mind?" Hailey asked, suddenly realizing she should have probably asked for a few more details before agreeing to the deal.

Before Santa could respond, Hailey was distracted by a mom with two kids walking by. The boy looked to be about five years old and kept pulling on his mom's hand, urging her in Santa's direction. The little girl was probably two and was hiding behind her mom's legs, gazing suspiciously at the entire Santa display. Hailey smiled encouragingly at the mom and kids. *Oh please, let them come!* She begged the mom silently. There was no way they were going to get over a hundred visitors, but a few here and there to pass the time would be more than enough for Hailey.

As the mom's eyes crossed Hailey's friendly expression of welcome, she relented and brought both children to Santa's corner.

"Is there a fee for letting them see Santa?" she asked hesitantly.

"No, not at all," Hailey replied. "I will snap a picture and give you a little printed proof. Then you can order pictures later if you want. There are some toys, candy, and other merchandise for sale in the corner by the cash register, but visiting Santa is completely free."

At his mom's nod, the little boy excitedly climbed into Santa's lap and began spouting off a very impressive Christmas list. Hailey hurriedly snapped the picture. While the proof printed and Santa conversed with his little friend, Kaden, Hailey did her best to remember and write down in her notebook the major points of Kaden's list. Tearing the page out of her notebook, she handed both it and the proof to the mom, explaining that she knew that Santa's helpers sometimes needed a little assistance in remembering the details of a list.

The mom smiled her thanks, and then urged her shy toddler over to Santa. After a few soft words and smiles from both Santa and Hailey, the little girl was soon contentedly sitting in Santa's lap. While she wasn't exactly smiling in the picture Hailey snapped, she did have the most adorable look of fascination as she gazed up at the jolly man holding her.

After handing her the little girl's proof, the mom relented yet again and, along with placing an order for pictures right then, she also purchased the small Santa bobble head doll her son had fallen in love with. For her daughter, she bought a pretty little elf figurine that looked almost like a fairy.

As Hailey totaled her purchases, she saw Kaden happily bouncing around and shaking the bobble head, surely giving the poor doll irreversible whiplash.

Pausing in fishing her credit card from her wallet, she called, "Kaden, settle down and come over here please before you break something."

Kaden either didn't hear or didn't want to hear. He kept spinning, dancing his new bobble head while he hummed 'Rockin' Around the Christmas Tree.' Not looking where he was going, the doll suddenly smacked into one of the pillars surrounding the Christmas display. Santa's head flew off, never to bobble again. Kaden immediately burst into tears.

Finished with her transaction, his mom walked over and picked up the pieces.

"Kaden, I told you to settle down! I'm sorry, but I can't get you a new one. Maybe Daddy can fix it when we get home. Next time, maybe you can remember to listen."

With tears streaming down his heartbroken face, Kaden was inconsolable as his mom took his hand and urged him away. Hailey knew that there was no way his dad would be able to patch bobble head Santa back together again. From seeing the impact, Hailey knew the little doll's injuries were not ones that could be recovered from.

Hailey couldn't take it. Not when she could do something about it.

"Excuse me," she called. "If you wouldn't mind, Kaden can have a replacement Santa at no extra charge. These bobble heads don't seem very study, and I know accidents happen sometimes. It seems like I'm always messing up like that too."

At the mom's look of gratitude and nod of consent, Hailey handed Kaden a new bobble head. Kaden's sobs came to a sudden halt and joy dawned over his face like a beautiful rainbow after a storm.

"Now be really careful of that one. He's probably like the other one and rather fragile. You'll have to take good care of him. And it's also important to remember to listen to your mom and obey her the first time."

After Kaden and his mom's profuse thanks, they finally left. Hailey promptly dropped the broken bobble head in the trash and got her wallet out of the bottom drawer in the checkout stand. Ringing up another purchase of a bobble head Santa, she placed her own cash into the register to cover the cost of Kaden's replacement.

Finishing, she turned to find Santa's eyes watching her every move.

"Now at least my inventory count won't be screwed up," she said casually.

The look on Santa's face was rather intense and seemed almost like admiration, but his focus was making her feel extremely self-conscious. She began needlessly rearranging merchandise, poinsettias, and other Christmas décor.

"You're really good with kids," Santa finally said

"I should be. I am a teacher," Hailey answered. Then, with a grimace, she amended, "Or rather, I was a teacher."

"What happened?"

Hailey sighed. Santa sure was nosey, but she didn't really care. If he wanted to listen to at least part of her sob story, at least it would pass the time. "I was a first grade teacher up until about three months ago. The school I was working at had an unexpected shortfall in the budget. Since I was the teacher most recently hired, I was laid off right before school started. Unfortunately, it was too late for me to get another teaching position. I've been substitute teaching, but it looks like I'll have to wait until next year to get another teaching position."

"So how did you come to be dressed in an elf costume?" Santa asked with a smile.

"I don't get called to substitute every day. In order to pay the bills I got a sales job here at the store. My shift is usually nights and weekends, so it works well with substituting. But when Jerry offered me the position as an elf over the Christmas season, I couldn't turn it down. I make more money than I usually do in sales, and it's something different. I don't like sales. I actually worked as an assistant in a photography studio when I was in college, so Jerry liked that I had some experience, though this is the first time that I've done it with bells on, literally."

"I bet you are a really good teacher. You completely light up when kids are around."

Hailey shrugged and unexpectedly felt the burn of tears behind her eyes. "I miss it," she said simply. Needing to get the attention off herself, she tried to shift the focus. "You seem pretty good with kids yourself. You were great with that shy little girl."

Santa shrugged. "I have a lot of nieces and nephews. While I don't have any professional experience like you, I am an expert at spoiling them, which seems to be a good skill to have when representing Mr. Claus."

"And just how did you manage to land such an important job," Hailey quipped. She had answered enough questions. It was his turn to answer a few of hers.

But the question died and was completely forgotten as soon as it left her lips. For at that second, she looked up and saw what seemed like a wall of children. It looked as if all of Disneyland had just evacuated, and every child was now coming to see Santa.

CHAPTER 2

With eyes wide and mouth agape, Hailey looked at Santa. They were about to be swamped by what she could only estimate was well over a hundred eager children. Santa shot her a look back, his bearded mouth twitching in a grin and his eyes dancing merrily in what could only be described as pure orneriness.

And Hailey knew. *He set me up! He knew this was going to happen!*

Before Hailey had a chance to interrogate the suspect, they were bombarded by children excitedly vying for their turn on his lap. The next few hours passed in a blur as Hailey frantically performed her duties as elf. She positioned kids, took pictures, sold merchandise, and still somehow managed to write one or two Christmas list requests on a notebook page for each child. Just when it seemed the line was finally getting shorter, a new group of at least fifteen four year olds would arrive and wait their turn.

At 6:00, the last child had sat on Santa's lap and left, returning the display area to its former empty state. Hailey immediately began balancing the cash register while Santa straightened up and returned equipment to its proper place. Finishing before Hailey, he came over, leaned on the counter, and watched her finish counting the day's income.

"Stop watching me," she ordered. "You're making me nervous."

"Then hurry and finish up," Santa replied. "We have a bet to settle."

Amazingly, Hailey managed to balance the money to the penny, matching it exactly with the receipts from the day. That never happened on the first try. Not wanting to jinx it by checking her math again, she quickly slid the printed paper in a bank bag along with the money.

After firmly zipping it closed, she looked up at Santa. "113. That's how many children visited the Santa corner today. How did you know that over a hundred kids would be coming?"

"I counted 115, but I guess it doesn't matter," Santa said, his eyes sparkling with feigned innocence. "What makes you think I knew we would have that many kids? You almost make it sound like I tricked you into our little bet."

"Didn't you?" Hailey asked, directly challenging his gaze with her own.

Santa's grin turned a little sheepish as he finally admitted, "I saw the schedule. Jerry showed me. I knew preschool classes were scheduled to visit today, and I saw the expected numbers."

Hailey felt aggravated. Jerry was the manager. Why hadn't he mentioned the schedule to her? She'd had no idea.

"So that's why we opened so early," Hailey said. "Why didn't Jerry tell me? And why didn't you tell me when I was ranting about opening before Thanksgiving?"

"I can't speak for Jerry; I just know it worked to my advantage to not tell you. After all, you lost the bet. You owe me a date."

Hailey flashed him a look of annoyance.

"You aren't going to back out are you? We had a bet."

"But you cheated!"

"I did not! I just never mentioned that I already knew how many kids would be coming. And you never asked."

Hailey realized he was right. As bizarre as it sounded, she had been tricked fair and square.

"Fine!" she said, relenting. "What exactly did you have in mind for me to pay off my debt? What kind of 'date' are we talking about?"

She was suddenly extremely nervous. What had she gotten herself into? She didn't even know this guy's real name. When they had first met, Hailey had introduced herself, but Santa hadn't, simply diverting the conversation in a different direction. Now she was locked in to going on date with a man she didn't even know.

"Relax, Hailey. It's not as if I'm some kind of ogre."

Hailey raised her eyebrows, as if questioning his statement when considering that he had obviously tricked her into a date with him.

"Okay," he acknowledged. "How about we make this as nonthreatening and painless for you as possible? Public place. Lots of people. You can even meet me there."

Hailey nodded skeptically. She wasn't going to trust him again until she knew all the details of what he was proposing.

"If you be my date for the company Christmas party, we'll call everything even."

"But the party isn't until December 23! That's a month away!"

"Is that a problem?"

Hailey was the type of person who liked to get unpleasant tasks over as quickly as possible. She would have been so relieved if he would have considered it a full payment to go out to coffee right now. On the other hand. the company Christmas party wasn't much to ask. It probably couldn't even be considered a real 'date.' There would be lots of other people attending and no possible expectations of romance or anything besides companionship. If she complained about his plan, he might change his mind and up the terms.

"Okay, you have a deal. I'll be your date for the Christmas party."

"Thanks, Hailey." Santa paused. "I promise I'm not some weirdo. I'm just a normal guy, and I happen to like you."

Slightly embarrassed, Hailey broke eye contact and took her purse out of the bottom drawer. If he was a normal guy, why hadn't he told her his name and asked her out like normal guys usually do when they like a girl?

Hailey took her Santa list notebook and stuffed it in her purse.

"Why do you do that, Hailey?" Santa asked, gesturing to the notebook. "Why do you write down the kids' Christmas lists? It's not like you aren't already busy. It's not required. I've been playing

Santa for several years now, but I've never seen another elf do that. It's really going above and beyond."

Hailey shrugged. "I figure it's probably hard for the parents to remember what their kids said. My sister has three kids, and in a chaotic situation like this, she has trouble keeping track of her kids' names, let alone trying to remember the sometimes shocking requests they tell Santa."

"That's really sweet of you, Hailey."

Hailey felt a warm blush start as she once again read the admiration in his eyes.

The moment ended as she heard her cell phone beep from her purse. Taking it out, she read the text message from her sister: 'Issues with Spencer. ETA?' If Jamie was asking when she'd be home, then things must be really bad with her son, Spencer.

"I've got to go," she told Santa, moving past him. "I'll see you later."

"Are you working tomorrow?" he asked.

"Yes," she said, turning around to answer him but continuing to back up. "It's the same shift as today."

"Me too. There are more preschool classes on the schedule. Then Friday we'll probably start having the normal holiday crowd."

"Yeah, I don't think I'll be making any more bets with you any time soon."

"I don't know," Santa said, his bearded mouth twitching with humor. "I'm sure we can think of something to pass the time and make things more interesting."

Hailey smiled and waved briefly before hurrying out the door. Maybe it was just a testament for how bad things were going in her life, but she found herself almost looking forward to work tomorrow.

*****

Hailey glanced at her watch as she hurried through the door. She wasn't late, but she was cutting it closer than she liked. She felt pretty conspicuous walking through the store in her elf costume, but right now, she was thankful she'd changed before she'd left home. Sure, it was a little embarrassing to walk around dressed like an elf, but it was better than to risk being late.

It was the call from Spencer's school that had delayed her. She'd had to call Jamie at work and let her know that Spencer was in the principal's office again. Jamie had been understandably upset. Ever since her husband had left her for another woman, she had been struggling with trying to manage her own broken heart and her children's confusion. Spencer had been acting out at home, and now it appeared to be spreading to school. Though Hailey had moved into her sister's home to help out, she was well aware that she could never fully ease her sister's burden.

Hailey rushed through the maze of merchandise, the silly bells on her hat and shoes jingling merrily.

She would have to bypass the Santa display to swipe her time card in the employee section by the store management offices. At least she could let Santa know she was here, but she wouldn't be able to take time to say more than that. She only had about three minutes before she would be officially late.

She was sure there would be plenty of time later to interrogate Santa. It seemed ridiculous to her that she didn't know what he looked like or anything about him. Yet he'd made it obvious that he liked her. And by the way she'd been anticipating work, she knew that, for some reason, she kind of liked him too. So today she wasn't going to accept subject changes or diversions. She was determined to get more information out of him, such as his name, for starters.

Hailey's calves burned as she careened around the corner of yet another display kiosk. Suddenly she stopped. As her eyes collided with the Santa's corner, she felt her mouth fall open in shock.

There was another elf in the corner. She was cute, young, and blond, and she was smiling flirtatiously while leaning close to Santa—her Santa.

CHAPTER 3

Santa spotted her and jumped up from where he was seated on the Santa throne. "Hailey, there you are! Jerry wants to see you. He said to tell you to come to his office immediately."

"Okay," Hailey replied, more than a little dazed and confused. She mechanically headed toward the offices hidden behind the back Christmas façade.

What was going on? Had she been replaced? There was only supposed to be one elf assigned to the Santa corner. Maybe Jerry just needed to assign her elsewhere for the day. But the blond elf currently standing in the Santa corner was too young, too cute, and far too perky for Hailey to feel any sort of job security. In fact, as she watched Santa smile at something the elf said, Hailey actually felt what could only be described as purely irrational jealousy.

Hailey went directly to the back offices, but before she could knock on the manager's door, a voice interrupted her.

"You'll have to wait a few moments, Miss Rhodes."

Hailey turned around to find Jerry's administrative assistant sitting at her desk. Hailey had completely bypassed her in her single-minded quest to get some answers.

"Oh, I'm sorry," Hailey replied. "I was under the impression that Mr. Simms was expecting me."

"He is, but he got delayed. If you'll just have a seat for a few minutes, I'm sure he will be with you shortly."

Hailey obediently sat in one of the functional, yet highly uncomfortable, chairs outside Jerry's office As the administrative assistant, Tilda, got back to work, Hailey realized the prognosis was getting worse by the second. If Jerry was intending to reassign her for the day, he wouldn't be making her wait. Her shift should be beginning right now. He wouldn't want her wasting time waiting for him. If he was unavailable, he would just leave a message for her with Tilda. No, there had to be something more serious that Jerry wanted to discuss with her.

The minutes slowly ticked by. Hailey felt ridiculous, nervously sitting there in her pointed elf hat and shoes. Finally, Hailey realized that there was one thing she couldn't wait for any longer.

"Excuse me, Tilda, but I need to use the restroom really quick. I'll be right back."

Hailey didn't know if it was from an actual sense of urgency or just nerves, but she made a beeline for the restroom without even waiting for Tilda's response.

Feeling much better when she emerged a few minutes later, she reclaimed her chair, but she was there less than thirty seconds when Jerry's door finally opened.

"Come on in, Hailey," Jerry said, sticking his head out the door.

Nervously, Hailey followed him into the office. As was his habit when meeting alone with any employee, he left the door open to the outer office. Tilda would be able to clearly hear whatever it was Jerry planned to say to her. She wracked her brain, trying to think of what possible reason Jerry might have for wanting to see her. She hadn't broken any rules that she knew of. She hadn't been late or missed a shift. But none of her reasoning eased the strong sense of foreboding that churned her stomach.

At his gesture, Hailey took the chair in front of his desk while Jerry positioned himself in the massive chair behind the desk.

After making sure he had her attention, he slid a small piece of paper across the smooth desktop.

"Here is your check, Hailey. I'm sorry to say that we will no longer be needed your employment. We have to let you go."

"But why?" Hailey choked out. "Did I do something wrong?" Even though she had suspected something major, she didn't think she'd be fired. Shock coursed like electricity down her limbs.

Jerry grimaced. "You're not being fired, Hailey. Just laid off. I even included a little severance pay. It turns out we are over-staffed and have to eliminate some positions."

"Over-staffed? That doesn't make sense! It's the holiday season! You just hired a bunch of seasonal employees. That elf who replaced me out there is probably one of those seasonal employees. Is she even out of high school?" Hailey knew she was getting worked up. Having an attitude and saying things she would later regret wouldn't get her job back, but she was so upset; she felt almost helpless to stop her emotions and the torrent of words.

Jerry sighed, "Okay, Hailey, if you want the technical explanation, here it is. When a company is trying to cut costs, one of the ways they can do that is to eliminate permanent positions in favor of temporary ones. With the economy the way it is, we currently have too many employees for the majority of the year. Seasonal workers are less expensive and don't require the benefits that a Grant's employee does."

"But why me? I need this job, Jerry! I don't understand. Just last week you told me how glad you were that I had photography experience and wouldn't need any additional training before starting in the Santa corner. Now you're telling me that I'm not needed?"

"There's nothing I can do, Hailey. Everything I said to you was true, but I have no say in this matter. The decision came directly from the top, and I'm sure it was just based on your numbers. Yes, you are highly over-qualified for this job, but on paper, your performance doesn't look so great."

At Hailey's look of confusion, Jerry continued. "Look, I assigned you to work the Santa corner for the holiday season, but your official job description is sales. Your sales numbers aren't as high as the other employees. I know that's because you refuse to pressure customers, and I've overlooked it because you're well-liked, a great leader, and have other skills, such as photography. But your sales methods haven't exactly produced impressive results. You are also the most recent hire in the sales department. It wasn't my choice, Hailey. But there isn't anything I can do about it."

Hailey bowed her head as a wave of hopelessness washed over her. There was nothing she could do. Straightening, she reached and took the paycheck off the desk. She bit her lip and furiously blinked her eyes, trying to hide her reaction from Jerry.

"I'm really sorry, Hailey," Jerry said, apparently seeing through her brave façade. "I know you've had a run of bad luck lately—first losing your teaching position and now this one. I wish there was something I could . . ." Jerry paused, and, as if suddenly having an idea, he began shuffling through the papers on his desk. "I just this morning saw an announcement about Grant's corporate office needing to immediately hire a buyer for our children's department. Something happened and left the position unexpectedly vacant. They need someone right away to complete the transactions before the end of the year."

"Thanks, Jerry, but there's no way I would qualify for a position like that."

"You don't know that. It's worth a shot. If I remember, you have a minor in Business, right? With that and your experience with children, you might be able to do it. Why don't you give me your resume, and I'll turn it in along with a good word."

"You already have my resume," Hailey replied wearily. "I gave it to you when I was hired a few months ago. I guess not much has changed on it since then."

"Okay, I'll have Tilda find it in your file, and I'll forward it to the right person."

Seeing no reason to sit and wait until Jerry located what he was looking for, Hailey stood, thanked Jerry, and left the room. If it made Jerry feel better to forward her resume, then Hailey figured it would be fine. She knew that the reality was that, even with his good recommendation, she had no chance of getting a job like the one he described. She had no education or experience that would qualify her. In fact, she was sure that her resume would be immediately filed into file 13, otherwise known as the trash.

Hailey didn't even look at Tilda as she walked through the outer office. Tilda probably knew that she had been canned. She always seemed to know those things, and Jerry's open-door policy didn't lend itself to privacy. Hailey didn't mean to be rude, but she was afraid that if there was any sympathy or understanding in the office assistant's eyes, she would lose her fragile hold on her emotions and have a meltdown.

"Best of luck, Miss Rhodes," Tilda's voice called quietly as Hailey made her exit.

Hailey practically gagged on what could only be described as the combination of a half-sob and a half-laugh. Luck! That was one thing Hailey did not have!

Hailey walked quickly back through the Santa corner, trying not to even glance in the direction of Santa and his new elf. She just wanted to get out of there! The once-merry sound of the bells on her pointed shoes now seemed to mock her. She would have to return the costume to the store later--that is, if she didn't burn the garment first. She didn't have any clothes to change into now, so she would have to just deal with the taunting music of the tiny silver bells.

"Hailey," she heard Santa call her name, but she didn't pause. "Hailey, wait!"

She pretended as if she hadn't even heard him as she made a beeline out of sight. She needed to get home and somehow break the news to her sister. She was filled with dread at the thought of that conversation. Jamie had already been through so much, and now Hailey wouldn't be able to help her with the bills.

She certainly didn't need to stop and spill her guts to some guy in a Santa suit. She didn't even know his name. No, he could turn his charm on her perky little elf replacement. Maybe he could take *her* to the company Christmas party.

As difficult as it was to make a dignified exit in an elf costume, Hailey felt she managed fairly well. But as she located her car in the parking garage, reality pressed in on her, and the tears began. It was difficult to say which thought upset her most: her unemployment, the looming conversation with her sister, or the thought of Santa with someone else.

CHAPTER 4

The phone rang.

Ugh. "Jamie, are you going to get that?" Hailey called.

No answer. The phone continued ringing.

Hailey was lying on the couch, staring blankly at a black and white movie on TV. She never wanted to move again. It had been such a horrible day, and after helping Jamie get her three kids in bed, Hailey was so physically and emotionally exhausted, she didn't know if she could get up enough energy to drag herself upstairs and get herself ready for bed as well. Now the phone was ringing and Jamie was ignoring it, probably just expecting Hailey to get it. Maybe she should just let the answering machine pick it up. No, 9 times out of 10, people wouldn't leave a message, and it would drive Hailey crazy to wonder who had called.

With a grunt, she rolled off the couch, jumped up, and sprinted to grab the phone off the counter before the machine picked it up on the sixth ring.

"Hello?"

"Hi . . . Hailey?"

"Yes, this is Hailey." Who was this? Hailey strained to place the voice. She was really bad at identifying voices on the phone. Anybody who knew her made a practice of identifying themselves early. Otherwise, Hailey could go the entire conversation thinking they were someone else.

"This is . . . Santa. You know, the guy you worked with yesterday at Grant's?"

"Oh. Hi." Suddenly, Hailey snapped out of her shock. "Wait a minute! How did you get my phone number? I never gave it to you."

"I got it from Jerry."

"Jerry? Why would he give it to you? Isn't that some kind of breach of privacy or something?"

"Jerry wanted me to call you to see if you'd be interested in working with me for the Downtown Dazzle at Fountain Square. You know, the big party they do downtown for the Christmas season. We would be scheduled for the first Saturday in December. It's just this one time gig, but Jerry thought you might be willing to do it since . . ."

"Since I'm unemployed and desperate," Hailey finished. "Sure, I'll do it." Really what choice did she have? Every little bit of income would help. "I was planning on going to the party with my sister and her kids anyway. What time am I supposed to be there?"

"The music will start at 5:45, but as long as you're there before 6:30, you should be fine. Events end at 8:30. Jerry said you already had the elf costume, but . . ."

That was stating it tactfully since she had walked out of the store with it on.

"You'll actually need to go by the store and exchange it for a different one," he continued, his tone a little hesitant.

Hailey felt suddenly wary. What exactly had she just agreed to?

"What kind of costume are we talking about?" Hailey asked suspiciously.

Santa hesitated, but then admitted in a rush. "Mrs. Claus. After the fireworks, kids can have cookies and do a craft with Mrs. Claus. There is already a Mrs. Claus lined up for the other Saturdays in December, but not for this one. You don't have to plan anything. The craft is completely prepared. You just have to dress in the costume and be great with kids like you usually are. Please, Hailey, don't back out now."

Hailey sighed. "I'll do it. I could really use the money. And could dressing as Mrs. Claus be that much worse than wearing an elf costume?"

Santa laughed. "Thanks! It'll probably end up being a lot fun. Just make sure you dress warm under your costume. Every year they do this Downtown Dazzle the first three Saturdays in December. It's very popular, but I have no idea why they do it at night. December in Cincinnati is way too cold."

"They do it for the atmosphere," Hailey replied. "It's so much more romantic and Christmasy with all the lights and ice skating in the dark."

"I guess. Oh, and I wanted to tell you about a possible teaching position I heard about. My niece and nephew go to a private school. A teacher isn't returning after Christmas due to some health issues, so the school is going to be looking for another teacher to fill the position. If you email my sister your resume, she said she'd make sure it gets to the right people."

Great. Another guy trying to connect her with a job she had no chance of getting.

"If you give me her email, I'll send the resume," Hailey said, somewhat wearily. "But usually private schools have strict requirements for teachers. I doubt I would qualify. You just about have to have a degree in paperwork to just fill out their novel-sized application, not to mention the letters of recommendation and other prerequisites."

"You never know unless you give it a try. I think they're pretty desperate to get a good teacher, and from what I've seen, you'll have no problem fulfilling that requirement."

Hailey obediently wrote his sister's email on a tablet that had been left on the counter by the phone. She knew this job would be another dead end, but she might as well at least humor Santa.

The conversation stalled, uncomfortable silence stretching over the line.

"Well . . . thanks for calling about the jobs," Hailey said, not knowing what else to say.

"No problem," he replied. "But I have to admit something. Jerry wanted me to call about the job, and I thought I would mention the teaching position; but, I also had ulterior motives."

Hailey felt the pace of her heart quicken.

"I wanted to make sure you were okay. I was worried when you left the store so suddenly yesterday."

Realizing the conversation wasn't wrapping up as she had anticipated, Hailey walked back over and flopped on the couch.

"I'm okay," Hailey lied.

"No you're not," Santa shot back. "You just lost your job for the second time in a few months. It's the holiday season, and I'm sure this has shot a hole in whatever plans you had."

"It definitely makes things more difficult," Hailey admitted. Then, having no clue why she was opening up to this man she didn't know, she continued. "I live with my sister so I can help her out. Jamie's husband left her for another woman about eighteen months ago. He's pretty much a scum bag. He hasn't paid any child support or even come to see their three kids since then. Our parents live in Florida and weren't able to help, so I left my teaching job in Michigan and moved back here to help Jamie. She has had a really hard time emotionally, financially—with just about everything. I got a job teaching first grade last year, but then, well, you know what happened there."

"Wow, that's got to be really tough."

That was an understatement. But Hailey wasn't going to spill all of her guts. She wasn't going to talk about how difficult things were for Jamie. Or about how Hailey had been helping Jamie with everything from the rent to parenting. Now, in addition to the other chaos in her life, Jamie felt incredible guilt for what she saw as taking Hailey away from a job she loved in Michigan only to have her lose two jobs here in Cincinnati. Hailey in no way resented her sister, but it was impossible to talk Jamie out of her feelings.

"I guess," Hailey replied. She really didn't have a desire to get into a deep conversation right now. Not only did she not know the person on the other side of the line, but she didn't think she could emotionally handle dissecting her feelings and the recent events in her life.

Instead, she tried to put a lighter spin on things, saying, "It's pretty difficult to feel too mad at life when watching 'It's a Wonderful Life' on TV."

"That's funny. I'm looking at that same movie on my TV as well. Gotta love Jimmy Stewart. And the movie has such a great message."

"I've always liked it," Hailey agreed.

She should've just said 'good night,' and ended the conversation. But she wasn't ready to go to bed. She really disliked watching a movie alone, but she knew Jamie wasn't going to come back downstairs. Jamie had gotten into another argument tonight with her fourteen year old son, Spencer. With Spencer's behavior added to the news of Hailey losing her job, she knew Jamie would probably shut herself in her room and cry herself to sleep. That's what she usually did when upset. She just didn't realize that Hailey knew about all those nights. It was hard to miss the soft sobs when Hailey passed her sister's bedroom door. And the red-rimmed, puffy eyes in the mornings were rather obvious as well.

On the surface, Jamie had taken Hailey's news very well. But then Jamie usually approached life with a very calm veneer. Hailey had long ago learned to see beyond the face Jamie presented to the world. She would have loved to comfort her sister, but Jamie would never allow it. She would reluctantly accept Hailey's help as necessary for her children, but she would never accept Hailey's help for her personally. She insisted on shedding her tears privately. So Hailey was left not wanting to face yet another night alone.

And so, she opened her mouth and shared her thoughts with a department store Santa Claus.

"I don't know that I've ever thought that the world would have been better off without me, but I can definitely relate to George Bailey's desperation of not knowing why a bad situation has happened and not seeing a way out of it."

Drat! She needed to gag herself! She hadn't wanted to get into a serious conversation. At least she hadn't said everything that had been on her mind lately.

"Are you a Christian, Hailey?" Santa asked, somewhat abruptly.

"Yes I am," she replied. "I was saved as a child and grew up in church. My faith in God is still priority in my life, though I won't pretend it's always easy."

"I thought you probably were a Christian. Sometimes you can tell by the way someone acts. At least, that's what we Christians hope. But with you, you're actually successful at showing Jesus by your actions."

Hailey was a bit speechless. She didn't remember if she'd ever received such a compliment.

"Anyway, since you're a Christian, you know that God has a plan for your life even if you can't see it now. Things will work out, Hailey."

"Knowing it and feeling it are two entirely separate things."

"That is very true. That's why you need people around you to help you remind your feelings to shape up and match what you know."

That's easier said than done, Hailey thought. She really thought she had been doing God's will when she'd moved back to her hometown of Cincinnati to help Jamie. But things had gone from bad to worse for her. She knew that being a Christian and being a good person in no way guaranteed one wouldn't have difficulties. However, on at least some level, she felt like she deserved better than this! If she was doing God's will, shouldn't He be keeping this sort of thing from happening to her?"

"The story isn't over yet, Hailey," Santa said softly, seeming to interpret her silence. "Things look bad now, but you can't see the whole picture like God can. You don't know how He can make good come out of your bad situation; you just have to trust that He will."

"Thanks for the encouragement," Hailey said. "I'll try to keep that in mind. Are you sure you aren't my Clarence? Maybe you're not really Santa as much as an angel trying to get his wings!"

Santa laughed. "I hope you're not disappointed, but no, I am far from an angel, even a slightly messed-up angel like Clarence. Unfortunately, I'm just a man, who happens to enjoy being Santa to little children and who had the luck, okay skill, to win a bet with his elf."

Hailey laughed. So he wasn't going to let her out of the bet even though she no longer worked at Grant's The thought of attending the Christmas party of her former employer still didn't sit well with her, but maybe she could find a way to amend their agreement later.

Hailey hadn't really been watching the movie before Santa had called. She'd just turned it on for background noise to try to distract her overactive mind. But now, she watched it 'with' the man on the other end of the phone line. He frequently inserted his own, often funny, comments and editorial review, while seeming to effortlessly draw Hailey out of her natural reserve. The time passed quickly, and before Hailey knew it, the credits of the movie were rolling.

With the sudden realization of how much she had talked and revealed about herself, Hailey felt embarrassed and somewhat exposed. She didn't know this man, and yet she had talked to him like they were long-time friends. Was she really that desperate for companionship and reassurance?

"What's your real name?" she asked suddenly. After telling the man practically everything about herself but her shoe size, she deserved to at least know his name!

There was silence. Hailey waited. Though she was more annoyed with herself than with him, she wasn't going to be distracted or let him off the hook this time. He was going to answer her question!

"Chris," Santa's voice finally answered softly. "You can call me Chris."

"You've got to be kidding me! Chris? As in Chris Cringle? I may as well just keep calling you Santa!

"That's your choice," he replied sweetly, his tone failing to hide his obvious enjoyment. "Chris or Santa is perfectly fine with me."

Hailey tried to be angry. Who was this man? But, for all of her effort, it wasn't working. Whether his name was Chris, Santa, or something else, she couldn't make herself care. At this moment, all she knew was that she liked him.

As Hailey struggled to formulate a response, Santa spoke again. "Thanks for talking to me and watching the movie. But I need to let you go."

Wait! Was he trying to make a quick exit to avoid more personal questions? That wasn't fair!

"Good night, Hailey," Santa said, laughter sounding in his soft voice.

Before she could come up with a way to stop him from hanging up, she found herself responding quietly, "Good night . . . Chris."

The line went dead. Sighing, Hailey clicked the 'off' button and stood to go upstairs. How pitiful was it that the best night she had in a long time was spent watching an old movie via phone with a man who, for all she knew, was still wearing a Santa suit!

As she passed by the counter, she grabbed her cell phone so she could plug it in upstairs. She had a voicemail. She looked at the time stamp on the message. It was before Chris had called. She had probably missed the call when she was helping four-year old Sylvie with her bath. Had Chris tried calling her cell phone first?

She played the message. It was a woman's voice.

"Hi. This message is for Hailey Rhodes. This is Andrea Holt with Grant's cooperate office. Your resume came to our attention via Jerry Solomon. I know it's late notice, especially with tomorrow being Thanksgiving, but I've been instructed to schedule an interview with you for Friday. You can call me back at this number. I'll be available tonight until about midnight. We're anxious to get the interviews scheduled and place someone in the position."

Less than five minutes after receiving the message, Hailey had an official interview scheduled at Grant's corporate office.

CHAPTER 5

"Hailey Rhodes?"

Hailey looked up to find a gorgeous man in a gray suit standing in the door of what she assumed was his office. Instant recognition hit her like a club, and her nervousness increased exponentially. She knew him.

Hailey quickly hopped out of her chair to meet the man with an outstretched hand and what she hoped was a confident smile.

"I'm Connor Montgomery," the man said, his steel gray eyes lighting up as he shook her hand. "I'm going to be conducting your interview today."

"It's nice to meet you," Hailey managed, hoping he wouldn't notice the quaver in her voice. She remembered him, but there was no way he would remember her. In reality, they probably had never actually spoken. But there was no way she would forget the most popular guy in high school, especially when he was also the same guy she'd had a monumental and thoroughly unrequited crush on. Besides, it didn't look like he'd changed at all in the years since high school. He was still tall and well-built with dark wavy hair and chiseled masculine features, but if anything, this man was much more attractive than the boy she remembered.

"Come on in."

Hailey followed him into the room. What was she even doing here? There was no way she would be hired for a job as a buyer for Grant's department store. She had just waited while two other professional-looking candidates had interviewed and exited this office with smiles on their confident faces. She should have never allowed Jerry to forward her resume for this position. She was not qualified at all, and now she was about to make a complete fool of herself in front of the breath-takingly handsome Connor Montgomery.

He gestured to a chair at a small conference table and moved to take his own seat opposite her.

"Miss Rhodes, this is Andrea Holt," he said introducing the woman also seated opposite Hailey. "I believe you spoke with her on the phone. As you know, we are interviewing for a buyer for our children's department here at Grant's. This position will have a lot of demands and responsibility as we are a nation-wide chain. I have been tasked with interviewing and hiring for this position, but the candidate we hire will report directly to Ms. Holt. She has assisted in scheduling, and I've also asked her to sit in on the interviews and provide her input, which will of course be considered in my final decision."

Hailey swallowed and resisted the urge to wipe her sweaty palms on her skirt. One glance at Andrea Holt and Hailey knew the woman didn't like her. Hailey remembered her saying that she had been 'instructed' to call Hailey for an interview, as if she wasn't doing it willingly. Her tone on the phone had been very cold, but now her dislike was obvious.

Ms. Holt looked to be in her early forties and was professionally dressed in an expensive-looking purple business suit. She would be very pretty with her artistically applied makeup and professionally applied artificial blonde, but the scowl on her face definitely detracted from her appeal.

"Miss Rhodes, could you please clarify exactly why you are applying for this job?" Ms. Holt asked abruptly. Apparently she wasn't going to waste any time with pleasantries.

"What do you mean?" Hailey asked, shocked at the woman's blunt approach and unfriendly tone.

Shouldn't she at least pretend to be nice? "I'm not sure what it is you're asking."

"What I mean is that, based on your resume, you obviously are not qualified for this position. Correct me if I'm wrong, but you have no experience as a buyer or really in business at all. The sum total of your background is a minor in Business, your history as a teacher, and a couple months in sales at one of our department stores. And, from what I've seen, you weren't very successful in your sales position! Is this accurate?"

When Hailey was younger, she would have been completely intimidated by Andrea Holt. She would have mumbled her way through the interview, apologized in every other sentence, and made a quick exit to sob her humiliation in private. But at some point, Hailey's attitude had changed. Maybe it was maturity or maybe it was just that, especially with all the bad things that had happened lately, she'd had enough.

Now, she was angry.

She didn't deserve this rude treatment. She had no idea why Ms. Holt disliked her, but it wasn't right to simply be hated on sight. Even if she wasn't qualified for this position, she deserved to be treated with respect.

"Hailey Rhodes . . ."

Hailey turned to see a thoughtful expression on Connor Montgomery's face. He had obviously not processed or cared what Andrea had just said.

"This may sound strange, but do I know you?" he asked. "You look very familiar for some reason."

"High school," Hailey answered flatly. Ms. Holt's rude attitude had instantly cured her insecurities and reservations. She wasn't in the mood to pretend to be clueless or play coy guessing games. The sooner she got this whole experience done with, the better. "You were a couple years ahead of me. I remember you because you were older, popular, and a star football player. I seriously doubt you remember me though."

"So you would have graduated with my sister, Carrie, right?"

"Yes. But I didn't know her well." She chose not to mention that his sister was in the popular crowd while she fell into more of the nerd group.

"Wait. Were you the valedictorian for your class?"

"Yes."

"I do remember you! You spoke at graduation. I remember being very impressed with your speech and thinking that my airhead sister would never come up with something like that."

Hailey normally would have reveled in the fact that he actually remembered her, but she was still too focused on Ms. Holt.

"Thank you," she replied. "I'm so glad it was memorable. And now, if I can address Ms. Holt's concerns . . ." Hailey turned her gaze back to the lady who was practically rolling her eyes with impatience at Conner's walk down memory lane. "You're correct in that I don't have an impressive resume, Ms. Holt. I am well aware that I don't have the education or work history that you would typically be looking for. However, I was urged to apply for this job based on my other qualifications. I was under the impression that you were looking for someone who could be successful in this position. Someone who knows children and would be able to identify products that would appeal to both them and their parents. Someone who is intelligent, a fast learner, and would represent the company well. If that truly is the person you're looking for, that someone is me."

Ms. Holt made a small noise that sounded suspiciously like a snort of disdain.

Out of the corner of her eye, Hailey saw Conner's eyes sparkling, as if he was thoroughly enjoying the scene and appreciated her response to the irascible Ms. Holt. He quickly stepped in and asked a few token questions about how she would handle aspects of the job. Mainly, though, he focused on her knowledge of children and how she could apply that to this job. Ms. Holt frequently threw her own sharp questions at Hailey like well-aimed darts, seeming to be purposely trying to make Hailey appear silly and inept.

Hailey rose to every challenge the other woman threw at her. She hadn't expected to get the job, but she had expected to be treated with respect. Ms. Holt's rude behavior lit a fire in her normally passive personality. She probably didn't even want the job as much as she wanted to put the woman in her place and not allow her to win.

After Hailey answered yet another of Connor's mild questions, Ms. Holt appeared to grow frustrated with the line of questioning, saying adamantly, "While your experience with children is admirable, Miss Rhodes, it does not make up for the fact that you are not qualified for this position."

"Then I apologize for wasting your time," Hailey replied, standing quickly from her seat. She could see now that there was no point to this interview, and she was rapidly tiring of the hostile situation. "I guess I was wrong about what you were looking for."

Hailey very much wanted to make one parting shot at Andrea Holt and throw back one of her own rude daggers, but she maintained her composure and managed a dignified exit from the room. She wouldn't get this job, but Hailey couldn't see that as all bad. At least she wouldn't have to work with that awful woman!

Hailey had escaped out the door before she realized Connor had followed her.

"I'll walk you down to the lobby," he said simply.

Hailey said nothing. Anger and adrenaline had left her trembling, and she just didn't think she could handle discussing high school memories with Connor.

As the elevator door closed, Connor spoke. "I'm sorry about Andrea's attitude. You should know that it isn't just you. She's rather intense with everyone and everything."

Hailey nodded.

"I'll give you a call when the decision has been made."

"Thanks, Mr. Montgomery. I really appreciate the opportunity."

"Hey, call me Connor. I still can't believe we ran into each other. I know we live in the same city we graduated in, but it's very rare that I encounter someone I knew from high school."

Hailey really didn't feel the need to remind him that he actually didn't know her from high school. She had been invisible to him.

She looked up at him, trying to think of some response, but Connor continued, "Maybe what's even more surprising is that I didn't notice you back then." The elevator doors opened and Connor grinned. "Trust me, I wouldn't make the same mistake twice."

Hailey felt a blush starting to spread across her face even as she doubted his words. She had no chance of getting the job, he would never call her about that or for any other reason, and, despite his flattering words, she would probably never see him again. Furthermore, it was very likely that he would never give her another thought.

Hailey's smile disguised her thoughts as she quickly said goodbye and tried to dismiss Connor as easily as he would dismiss her.

At least she had already emailed Chris's sister her resume for that teaching job at the private school. Not that she had any more chance of landing that job than she had this one. But at least all was not lost. She still had some unrealistic hope.

As she sat at home that afternoon searching the internet for jobs, the phone rang, and Hailey was forced to admit she'd been wrong. It was Connor Montgomery.

"Hi, Hailey, I'm calling to offer you the job as a buyer for Grant's children's department."

CHAPTER 6

Hailey looked up at the sound of someone knocking at her office door. Connor stuck his head in.

"Am I interrupting?" he asked, his friendly smile firmly in place.

"Yes," Hailey replied, returning her focus to the large stack of papers on her desk and trying not to be annoyed. Hopefully he had a good reason for being here. It was only her second day of work, and she was already so overwhelmed with the work load and trying to prove herself; she couldn't spare a single moment to shoot the breeze with Connor.

Seemingly unaware of her agitation, Conner sprawled in the chair in front of her desk as if it were a lazy summer day.

"I figured I was interrupting, but I couldn't resist," he said, unperturbed at her answer and tone. "I know you're overwhelmed, but I just wanted to tell you what a fantastic job you're doing. It's only Day 2, and even Andrea thinks you're doing well."

"No she doesn't!" Hailey shot back. "The woman absolutely hates me! She gives me orders and then wastes no time in informing me on every detail that I am not doing to her satisfaction."

"I know that's what it seems like, but I've talked to her. She actually has very little to criticize you about, which is driving her absolutely crazy! I love it! You probably have already figured out that Andrea did not want you hired. But it was my decision. It's giving me absurd delight that I was right about you, and she's as mad as a hornet. Not many people stand up to Andrea Holt."

"So did you hire me just to get under Andrea's skin?"

"Of course not! That's just an added benefit. I hired you because I thought you could handle the mess the other buyer left, and I thought you would do the best work. I did have to go against both Andrea's and Mr. Wright's wishes, but you're already proving that I was right about you."

"The CEO didn't want you to hire me?" Hailey asked, appalled.

Connor shrugged. "He only knew what it said on your resume. He left the final decision up to me."

It was more than a little unsettling that Connor was the only one who wanted her here. Both her boss and the big boss hadn't wanted to even give her a chance. Now she realized she would have to work even harder to prove herself capable.

"Well, I'm glad you don't think Andrea is getting ready to behead me for incompetence. You're right about the other buyer leaving a mess. Most of this paperwork is urgent and needs to be dealt with before the end of the year, but there doesn't even seem to be a system of organization for what needs to be done."

"Now you know why we were desperate to hire someone quickly."

"Thanks for your confidence in hiring me, but at this point, I'm not sure yet if it was deserved."

"You're doing great, Hailey, and you'll continue to do well. How about I take you to dinner sometime this weekend to celebrate your first week of work?"

Was he asking her out on a date? Hailey didn't go on dates very often. She didn't travel in many social circles that allowed her to meet nice, single guys her age. She felt so shocked that the handsome, successful Conner Montgomery might want to go out with her that she didn't know what to say.

"Is that even allowed?" she asked, spouting off the first thing that popped into her head. "I mean, we work together. I know some offices have a code of conduct against coworkers becoming involved."

Hailey felt her face heating up to a bright red. Why had she even brought it up? Maybe she was assuming too much. It was just dinner. It wasn't like he was asking her for a commitment.

"It's fine," Connor said confidently. The only rule is that personal relationships can't affect the work environment, but as long as relationships are kept separate and not pursued at work, they don't care. Besides, I'm not your boss. I hired you, but that was probably because Mr. Wright didn't trust Andrea to hire the best candidate. I rank higher than Andrea, but we're in charge of different departments. There's no conflict of interest in us seeing each other. So, what do you think, can I take you to dinner?"

Hailey felt her heart skip a beat, feeling momentarily like a sixteen-year-old girl who just got asked out by the star football player. Connor Montgomery was asking her on a date!

Hailey scrambled to find an appropriate response that didn't involve her jumping up and down excitedly. Not daring to make eye contact with Conner, her eyes fell on the large bouquet of red roses that graced her desk. She had received them yesterday with a card that had said, 'Congratulations on your new job.' In the space reserved for the sender's name was written 'Santa.'

Chris had called once over the weekend, and she had told him of her new job. They had ended up talking for over an hour. His sweet gift on Monday morning had completely thrilled her. And yet it was silly to imagine herself in a relationship with Chris. She didn't even know him. There's no way she should refuse Connor because she liked some mysterious man who hid behind a white beard and red velvet hat. But . . .

"I'm sorry, Connor, I already have plans this weekend," Hailey said, remembering that she was to help Chris at the Downtown Dazzle on Saturday. "Would your offer still be open for next weekend?"

"Of course! How about Saturday evening? That will give me a chance to get some great dinner reservations. It's such a busy time of year it's practically impossible to get a reservation anywhere but Dairy Queen."

Hailey smiled at his joke but felt the flutter of nerves as she realized that Connor might be way out of her league. She didn't remember the last time, if ever, she went to a restaurant that required reservations. Dairy Queen was much more her speed, and their Blizzard was fantastic. Would Connor be disappointed in her once he actually knew the kind of unsophisticated girl she was?

"Oh, there's Mr. Wright," Connor said suddenly. "I've got to hurry and get to that meeting."

Hailey's office had floor to ceiling glass along the front. She looked up to see a man with dark hair walk by with an entourage of other employees trailing behind. Mr. Wright was obviously a very busy man who was constantly in and out of the office. From what she had gathered, he was liked and well-respected by everyone, though she'd also heard he had high standards and expectations for his employees. It didn't bother Hailey that she hadn't met Mr. Wright yet, especially knowing that he'd been skeptical about hiring her. She would prefer to wait until she was more established and could feel more confident.

"We'll have to figure out the details for next Saturday at another time," Connor said walking to the door. I'll check in on you later, Hailey. Have a good afternoon. Get lots of work done so you can rub Andrea's nose in it." Turning back as he reached the door, he flashed his roguish grin, and nodded toward her desk. "Those are some nice flowers."

Hailey's eyes flew wide.

Connor shut the door to her office and rushed to his meeting.

Dazed, Hailey sat in her chair, picturing the look in Connor's eyes as he'd remarked on her flowers. How had she missed it before? The possibility seemed so obvious now. Was Connor Montgomery her Santa?

CHAPTER 7

Hailey stood on her tiptoes, scanning the crowd.

Where was he?

Chris had told her to meet him here at the Grant's display area at Fountain Square. She was in the right spot. She was right beside the skating rink. The decorations were in place. The tables were set up for the craft Chris had mentioned she would do with the children. She was even a little late. It was almost 6:30. Where was Chris?

Yes, she was short and there were thousands of people crowded into Fountain Square, but she really shouldn't be that difficult for him to find. As far as she could tell, she was the only person dressed so ridiculously in a Mrs. Claus costume.

Having exchanged her elf costume, Hailey now had to admit she might like this one even better. The mirror at home had reflected a very cute Mrs. Claus. Her pretty red and white dress was well padded and her blond hair securely tucked under a matching little red cap atop a soft white wig. The costume was complete with a pair of tiny spectacles that perched on her nose.

Now if she could just find her husband . . .

She checked her phone. No messages. No missed calls.

Christmas music filled the air from a choir's boisterous performance. With the music and the crowd, it was difficult for Hailey to concentrate and think clearly.

He had to be around here somewhere. He just didn't seem the type to stand her up as some sort of joke.

The choir ended their rendition of 'Here Comes Santa Claus.'

Some of the lights in the square suddenly went out. Hailey heard a murmur go through the crowd as the people stood shoulder to shoulder. They were all looking up.

Confused, Hailey followed their gaze. There was a spotlight on the top of the 525 Vine Building Office Tower. In the middle of the bright beam of light was a man dressed in a Santa suit! To Hailey's horror, he soon began climbing down the building! Then suddenly, he jumped!

Hailey's heart leapt in shock. An involuntary gasp went through the crowd. Then, as if lured by a magnet, Santa returned to the side of the building. Then, springing again, he shot down another few feet before his boots returned to solid safety once again.

Santa Claus was rappelling down the side of a building.

That couldn't be her Santa, could it?

Hailey remembered her sister mentioning something about the Downtown Dazzle last year, but Hailey had been so busy and stressed with all the Christmas activities for her class that she hadn't really paid attention. She had grown up in Cincinnati, but this definitely wasn't part of any celebration when she was a kid!

Hailey's breath caught in her throat each time Santa sprang away from the building. Part of her knew that he was safely attached to strong ropes, but she still couldn't help being afraid, especially when she saw that Santa wasn't alone in his rappelling feat. Two other people in reindeer costumes were rappelling with him. At some point, music over the loudspeakers had replaced the live choir. The movements of Santa and the reindeer almost appeared dance-like as they bounced around each other to familiar Christmas tunes.

The perky music did nothing for Hailey's taut nerves. She was sure the three would hit each other or get their ropes tangled, but they didn't. A jumbotron captured a close-up view of every agonizing detail of the descent. Though she tried, Hailey couldn't see enough details of Santa's face to identify him. With both humor and frustration, Hailey realized that she'd never be able to identify him, even if she could see his features! She didn't know what he looked like! Blue eyes was just about the extent of any description Hailey could come up with.

Though her head kept denying that the rappelling Santa was Chris, she was sure in her gut that he was. She couldn't bear to watch and couldn't tear her eyes away. What if something went wrong and Chris fell? Hailey had always been timid and adventures of the dangerous variety had never appealed to her. Each time Santa leapt away from the building, Hailey's heart leapt with him.

The trio delighted the entire audience, except Hailey, as they bounced their way down to land on the roof of a store lining Fountain Square. As Santa and his reindeer finally dropped from view, Hailey jumped at the sound of fireworks launching and lighting up the sky.

Moments later, Santa and the two reindeer appeared at the edge of the store roof, waving cheerfully to the crowd below. The fireworks show then officially began. The people oohed and aahed in all the right spots.

Hailey might have enjoyed the show except she realized that she was supposed to do her part right afterward. Frantically, she looked around. She knew she was to have cookies and do a craft with the kids, but she needed a bit more instruction than that! She looked at the tables. Maybe she could figure out the craft herself. Where would they put the supplies?

A deep voice right behind Hailey's shoulder made her jump. "You look beautiful tonight, Mrs. Claus."

Hailey whirled around to meet Santa's smiling eyes.

"Chris, what were you thinking, rappelling down a building? You could have been killed!"

Surprise flooded over his face, and then his bearded lips twitched in a slow smile. "You were worried about me?"

"Yes, I was worried about you! You could have died! And I certainly didn't want to witness Santa falling to his death!"

"Hailey, thank you for being concerned for me, but I was very safe. Every precaution is taken. We practice and rehearse beforehand. Not to mention the fact that I've been rappelling down that same building for years now—ever since we began this Downtown Dazzle."

The show was still going on, and it was difficult to speak in-between the booms of fireworks. Hailey opened her mouth to ask another question, but he interrupted her.

"We can talk more about it later, but right now, we're about to be accosted once again by a large number of children. Let me show you what the plan is."

Chris showed her where she would be positioned on a small platform to read a story, after which she would help distribute milk and cookies. Finally, she would be in charge of directing a craft. Thankfully, Hailey saw that the craft was well-organized and simple enough, and she was reassured when she saw several people in festive red costumes. Chris assured her that these other Grant's employees were there to assist.

Before she felt fully prepared, the show ended and children converged on their area. Hailey was soon reading 'The Night Before Christmas' to a large group. Hailey loved reading to children and soon felt herself relax into her role. After smiling, talking with her excited fans, and passing out what seemed to be thousands of cookies, she was once again speaking into a microphone to give instructions on the craft.

Each child was given a clear plastic bag with beads and string. They were to string the beads to make a small wreath ornament. In the middle of the wreath hung a tiny charm with the year on it. While she was helping string beads and tie knots, she would occasionally catch a glimpse of Santa helping with the craft or kneeling to hear yet another Christmas list. Hailey felt a rush of warmth at the sight of him. He was so patient and sweet with each child. There was very little Hailey found more attractive than a man who was good with kids.

In what seemed to be a surprisingly short time, Hailey noticed the crowd thinning out.

"Come on, Mrs. Claus," Chris said, appearing at her elbow. "Some little people are requesting an audience with us."

Chris led her back over to the platform where a line soon formed. The children waited to make their requests known to Santa while their parents waited for the photo-op.

Hailey looked up at the next children in line and was surprised to see her nieces and nephew. She knew her sister, Jamie, had planned to come tonight, but she really hadn't expected to see them with the thousands of people crowding downtown Cincinnati.

Knowing she needed to maintain her character, she resisted the urge to excitedly introduce them to Chris. She also resisted the urge to say something sarcastic to Jamie, who Hailey could tell was having difficulty keeping a straight face in her enjoyment over seeing her younger sister as Mrs. Claus.

Four year old Sylvie climbed up into Santa's lap. Jamie snapped a few pictures.

"Are you the real Santa?" Sylvie asked Chris, her blue eyes big.

"Of course he isn't!" Spencer snapped out before anyone else could answer. "He doesn't even look like Santa. Can't you tell that his beard is fake? Besides, you should know by now that there's no such thing as—"

CHAPTER 8

"Spencer!" Jamie said sharply, cutting Spencer off. "Stop it right now!"

Unfortunately Spencer's goal recently seemed to be to make everyone around him as miserable as he was.

"But he's right," eight year old Shaya said. "He isn't the real Santa, Sylvie, but Santa has lots of helpers this time of year. This Santa can let the real Santa know what you want for Christmas."

Sweet Shaya! She was the peacemaker and always trying to cover for her brother's bad behavior.

Having heard the exchange, another little girl standing in line spoke up, pointing directly at Hailey. "He might not be the real Santa, but I think she's the real Mrs. Claus. Look how short and fat she is. And she's really pretty and has white hair and everything."

Spencer, obviously intending to disagree and reveal exactly who Mrs. Claus was, said, "She's not—"

Hailey immediately shot her nephew her best teacher look, the one that was practically guaranteed to stop any misbehaving child in his tracks.

"Well, you might be right," Spencer mumbled as Hailey's fierce message was clearly received. "She might be the real Mrs. Claus."

"And her ears are pointed too," the little girl added, now thoroughly proud that she had been correct in her assessment. "Mommy, is Mrs. Claus part elf?"

Pointed ears? Were her ears pointed? Hailey resisted the urge to reach up to feel and reassure herself that the child was wrong. Instead, she turned her alarmed eyes to Chris, silently asking him to somehow contradict the offending statement. But she immediately saw that he would be no help at all as he was valiantly trying to hold in the gales of laughter at her expense.

Hailey heard the girl's mom appease her with an only slightly satisfactory answer. "I don't know, Sweetheart. Maybe she is."

The crisis now over, Shaya and Sylvie talked to Santa about their Christmas lists. While Spencer watched the whole scene with a scowl on his face, at least he was quiet and made no further comments.

As soon as the girls finished, Jamie quickly bustled her three children away. As she passed Hailey, she murmured a quiet, "I'll see you at home."

Hailey knew Jamie was feeling embarrassed over her son's behavior. Hailey felt bad. She would have liked to introduce Chris to her family, and she knew that Jamie had wanted to meet him after Hailey had filled her in on all the details of her mysterious Santa. Whereas Jamie was a private person, Hailey was much more open and freely shared the intricacies of her life with her older sister.

"That was my sister and her kids," Hailey whispered to Chris as the next child was coming forward.

He nodded his understanding.

A few minutes later, they watched as the last child walked away with a candy cane and a happy smile.

Hailey sighed. She was tired. It was already well past time the Downtown Dazzle was to have officially ended. Just a few Grant's employees remained cleaning up the area.

"I didn't realize we were also going to do Santa visits tonight," she said, moving to get down from the platform."

"It wasn't officially on the schedule," Chris said. "But it seems to happen every year anyway. The kids like to see both Santa and Mrs. Claus, and I never have the heart to tell them to come back during regular visiting hours."

Hailey looked at him, her eyes appraising. "You're a good Santa, Chris. Thanks for getting me the job tonight. It was fun."

"You're welcome. But we're not done yet."

"What do you mean?" Hailey asked, looking around. All the spectators were gone. People cleaning up and closing shops were all that remained. What did they still need to do?

"Come with me," Chris said, taking her elbow and guiding her to the skate rental counter at the edge of the skating rink. Though there were still a few people skating, the admission and rental were already closed for the night.

"Hey, Toby," Chris called. A young man with bright red hair popped his head up from where he'd been replacing skates on a bottom shelf. "Could we get a couple pairs of skates?"

"Oh, sure!" Toby said with a smile. "Anything for the big guy in red!"

"Uh, Chris, no!" Hailey said, immediately and thoroughly panicking. "I am NOT going skating!"

"Just consider it part of your job Hailey," Chris said with a smile. "Now, are you going to tell Toby your shoe size, or do I need to guess?"

Hailey reluctantly confessed to a size 7, and Toby set two pairs of skates on the counter.

Toby grinned at Chris. "You know, I tried to talk Keith into letting me put on the reindeer suit tonight, but he wouldn't go for it."

Chris replied, "If you really want to do it, Toby, we can get you trained for next year."

"Really?" Toby said. Even in the dim light, Hailey could see his eyes lighting up with joy. "You really think I could do the rappelling next year?"

"Sure!" Chris replied. "I'll mention it to the boss and get him to put you down for training. He's usually pretty cooperative about these things."

Toby laughed. "That would be great!"

"If you're gone before we're done skating, I'll return the skates sometime tomorrow if that's okay."

"Oh, sure! Have fun!

Toby returned to his work while Chris nudged Hailey over to a bench to put on the skates.

"Chris I really don't want to skate," Hailey again protested. Unfortunately, she knew the only chance of him listening to her was if she was completely, embarrassingly honest. "The truth is that I don't even know how to skate. I tried to go a few times as a teen with my youth group, but I almost did serious bodily injury to myself and others. It was not pretty. I think I resembled more of a bowling ball than an ice skater."

"You're in luck then!" Chris said enthusiastically, ignoring her protests. "I happen to be an excellent skater AND an excellent teacher."

Hailey locked eyes with him, letting him see the stark fear she was feeling. She did not want to do this! She did not want to skate, and she especially didn't want to do it in front of Chris! She hadn't been exaggerating. Hailey on skates was ugly and potentially hilarious to everyone but her. To her, it was humiliating.

Chris's teasing gaze turned serious. "Hailey," he said softly, reaching to take her cold hand in his. "It'll be okay. I won't let you get hurt or be embarrassed. It's the perfect time. There are only a few people skating. Besides, you're dressed as Mrs. Claus. You're not letting that embarrass you; why should you let this?"

Hailey took a deep breath. He was right. She tried to never let fear keep her from doing something. She'd just never had the opportunity to confront her mental block against ice skating. Worst case scenario: everyone would see Mrs. Claus making a fool out of herself. That wouldn't be so bad. Nobody would know it was her, and it may even give some lonely soul some comic relief.

Hailey laced up her skates and allowed Chris to lead her to the edge of the rink. She had a bad feeling about this. Hailey had never been accused of being graceful, and she would probably be even more off balance than usual since she was dressed in an ample Mrs. Claus costume. On the bright side, though, at least she would have plenty of padding!

Chris refused to give her time to think, pulling her quickly onto the ice. Pivoting, he securely held both of her hands in his warm ones and skated backwards as Hailey shuffled forward inch by inch.

"Hailey, look at me, not your feet," Chris ordered. "Trust me. I've got you. I'm not going to let you fall."

Hailey looked at him. He looked so ridiculous in his white beard. There was nothing about him that Hailey should find physically attractive, yet her pounding heartbeat couldn't be completely attributed to her fear. His hands in hers were warm and strong. His voice was gentle as he carefully instructed her in gliding with one skate then the other.

"You and your sister look alike," Chris said conversationally. "I figured out they were your family before you even mentioned it."

"Jamie is five years older than me, but people have always said we look alike, though obviously she's significantly taller."

"Well, you are part elf, remember?" Chris said with a smile.

Hailey rolled her eyes and resisted the urge to ask Chris about her ears. They were not pointed, and she refused to give him any enjoyment out of that comment.

"I'm sorry about Spencer," Hailey said, remembering the scene with a grimace. "He's had a lot of heartbreak lately and he's taking it out on the world."

"What's wrong?"

"Spencer has had a really difficult time since his dad left. He doesn't know the details about Steve taking off with another woman. My sister's really careful about not saying anything bad about Steve, hoping that he'll eventually want a relationship with his kids. Spencer has a lot of confusion and anger over it. We're not even sure where Steve is right now. So Jamie is on her own, trying to support three children, one of who has some serious anger issues over his dad leaving him."

"Jamie's not on her own," Chris said. "She has you."

"Except I don't seem to be much help lately. With losing my job twice, helping to pay the rent is a challenge. And I have no idea what to do about Spencer. It's not like we can afford to get him counseling." Hailey felt suddenly uncomfortable. *I shouldn't have mentioned all that! Talk about too much information!*

Hailey didn't usually share her personal problems. In her experience, people usually didn't want to know that much. Besides, it wasn't as if someone could make the situation better; mentioning it just made conversations awkward.

But Chris didn't seem to notice. "Is there something Spencer enjoys doing?" he asked. *It might help to give him an outlet for some of his anger if he was to be involved in something positive. It'd probably help him enjoy life more too.*

"He absolutely loves baseball, but this time of year there aren't a lot of options. There are a few academies and camps that have indoor leagues, but they're very expensive. Right now, Jamie's just trying to focus on having enough money so he can play in the spring."

To her surprise, Chris suddenly let go of one of Hailey's hands and moved to her side. She didn't fall! In fact, she was actually gliding almost gracefully! Her stride had lengthened from her initial shuffling, and she now felt the cold air whispering past her face as she smoothly skated around the rink. Hailey felt a thrill race through her. She was doing it! She now realized that Chris had been distracting her on purpose. With her mind off her feet, their movements had become automatic and gained confidence.

Hailey felt like she was flying! With Chris's hand in hers, she felt like she could—

Hailey's right ankle suddenly wobbled. Before she knew what was happening, her leg collapsed, and she crashed to the ice. As she fell, she kept hold of Chris's hand, her body swinging into his legs and knocking him down with her.

Hailey found herself looking up at the sky with a very large Santa on top of her.

CHAPTER 9

Before she could even assess whether or not she was hurt, Hailey started laughing. But with Santa constricting her lungs, she couldn't breathe, making her laughter resemble more of a croak.

Chris lifted his head and looked down at her, his eyes slightly disoriented and his jolly red hat askew.

"Hailey, are you okay?"

She had trouble speaking through her laughter. "Can't breathe . . . Get off me!"

Chris moved to her side, still looking at her with concern until he figured out that she was giggling almost hysterically. Then he joined her.

"I told you I was like a bowling ball!" Hailey said, tears streaming from her eyes in her merriment.

"I definitely would call that one a strike!" Chris shot back.

Still lying flat on the ice, Hailey looked over at Chris beside her. Suddenly, her laughter stopped. "Your hair is dark," she said, automatically reaching her fingers out to touch the dark waves escaping from under the Santa hat and attached white wig.

Chris shied away from her touch, leapt to his feet, and quickly readjusted his hat.

"Are you okay?" he asked, as if Hailey had never remarked about his wayward locks.

Hailey looked up at him in silence, finally accepting the hand he offered to help her up. Why did he not want her to know his true identity? Why the elaborate façade?

"I'm fine," Hailey replied, consenting to let the matter drop for now. "All of Mrs. Claus's padding softened my landing. What about you?"

"Same here. I guess this belly is good for a bit more than shaking like a bowlful of jelly when I laugh."

Now on her feet, Hailey hesitantly started skating again, though with considerably less freedom and speed than before.

"You are doing really well, Hailey. You may not ever earn a gold medal, but you'll surely be out of bowling ball status pretty soon. We'll have to schedule lesson number two soon, but remind me to wear my knee and elbow pads."

"You're not doing this next Saturday, are you?" Hailey asked suddenly, remembering the Downtown Dazzle wasn't a one-time event. She wouldn't mind a second ice skating lesson with Chris, but she knew she wasn't scheduled to work as Mrs. Claus next week. She didn't know which was worse: the thought of Chris rappelling down the building again or of that perky, young elf from the store playing his Mrs. Claus. "Don't they do the Downtown Dazzle for the first three Saturdays in December?"

"Yes, but I'm not the Santa for the other two Saturdays. I only ever do the first Saturday. It's all the time my schedule will allow."

"Your schedule? You work some place besides the store?"

"Of course!" Chris replied, his eyes crinkling with amusement. "Did you think being a department store Santa was the only thing I did?"

"How was I supposed to know? "It's not like you've given me any information about you at all."

Chris's features turned serious, and he acknowledged her statement with a nod. "I'm sorry, Hailey. I know it doesn't seem to be very fair, but I have my reasons for doing it this way. If you trust me, I'll eventually explain everything to you."

Hailey was silent as they skated, but she kept sneaking peeks at him out of the corner of her eye.

Her suspicions about his identity once again pushed to the surface. From the little she could see of him, he really did look like Connor. And Connor's hair was dark too. Hailey tried to remember Connor's voice. She was reasonably certain that it was deep and masculine, just like Santa's.

Chris sighed and, possibly thinking that she was upset, started talking. "Yes, I have a job that doesn't involve being Santa. Fortunately, they allow me some flexibility around the holidays so I can occasionally do a little work in the red suit. I do it because I like it. I like giving kids a little magic and joy. I started dressing up as Santa for my nieces and nephews. Then one day, I was in the right place at the right time. I was in a Grant's store and there was a long line of kids, but no Santa had shown up for work. So I put on the suit. After that, I was hooked."

"Thanks for telling me a little about yourself," Hailey said. Then, deciding to press her luck, she ventured a question. "How old are you anyway?"

Chris laughed. "What? Do I really look that old? You think I'm what, twenty years older than you?"

Hailey shot him a look of impatience and retorted, "At least." He was making fun of her serious question! She knew he said he had his reasons, but she still didn't understand his secrecy. It wasn't as if she was asking for his social security number!

"I'm in my early thirties, Hailey." Chris admitted. "Is that good enough? You're what, twenty-eight?

How was it that he seemed to know everything about her while she knew nothing about him!

Ignoring the fact that Hailey refused to respond, Chris said, "I'm going to be out of town on business off and on for the next two weeks. I'll try to call you, but I'm not sure how much time I'll have. Still plan on going with me to the Grant's Christmas party. You're not getting out of that one. Maybe we can do ice skating part 2 after Christmas."

Now he was talking about after Christmas? Their deal had only been for December 23rd.! But for some reason, Hailey didn't feel the need to remind him of that just now. She had enjoyed talking and spending time with him. She didn't know if she was ready to admit, even to herself, that she would miss him if he wasn't around for two weeks. Her date with Connor was scheduled for next weekend. But if her real Santa was going to be gone, maybe he wasn't Connor after all.

"I'd better be going," Hailey said as they skated to the edge of the rink. "Jamie will be wondering where I am. Besides, it's getting colder."

Reaching up, she rubbed her cold ears, trying to warm them up. "Some parts of me aren't nearly so well padded."

Are my ears really pointed? she thought, remembering the little girl's words.

Chris suddenly skated in front of her, blocking her progress so that she practically ran into him. He wrapped his arms around her to steady her balance. Chris was not a small man. Even with the suit on, Hailey could tell that his shoulders were broad and his frame well-muscled. She felt tingles that had nothing to do with the cold race up and down her spine. She felt small and protected in his embrace.

Gently, he drew her hands away from her ears.

Hailey started to ask him to give his honest opinion on the pointedness of the two little extremities, but he stopped her question with his gentle finger on her lips.

"Your ears are perfect," he said softly. "Thank you for tonight. Thank you for trusting me."

Hailey looked up into his eyes. It was too dark to see their blue color, but she was still transfixed by the way the lights of the skating rink danced in their depths.

She didn't know his full name, but he was in his early thirties. She didn't know where he worked, but for fun he liked to dress in a Santa suit and entertain children. He refused to reveal his identity or give away any personal details, but he fascinated her. In short, she still knew nothing about him. So why did she have the insane desire to pull his beard down and kiss him?

CHAPTER 10

Hailey looked at the menu and tried to hold down her panic. She didn't read French! She had no idea what the items were let alone how she was supposed to pronounce them to order.

She glanced up at Connor. He seemed perfectly at ease. She had been anticipating their date all week, but this was not at all what she had pictured. How could this man sitting across from her in a fancy French restaurant be her Santa?

But it had to be him. When Hailey had found out that Connor had been gone out of town on business all week, she knew she had been right. Connor was her Santa.

So why wouldn't he just admit it? He had to at least suspect that she knew. It was too obvious. Chris had admitted that he was gone, and then Connor was gone at the exact same time.

Connor looked up and met Hailey's eyes. "Would you like me to order for you, Hailey?"

"Yes, please," she said, relieved. "I have no idea what's good here."

Connor smiled, and Hailey felt like an idiot. It was an exclusive French restaurant. Everything was supposed to be good; that was the point, right?

The waiter arrived at their table, and Connor placed their orders for meals she couldn't hope to repeat, let alone pronounce.

"So I hear you have a big day on Monday," Connor said as the waiter left.

Connor had picked her up at her house, and so far, they'd only covered the topics of his Porsche and his recent trip to Italy. Though Hailey was very interested in Italy, she was relieved to be on a subject she knew something about.

"Yes. I'm supposed to give a big presentation to all the high-level executives about the status of the children's department, the changes I think need to be made, and the prognosis for the next year. It's a big job. I'm having to pull in a lot of data and resources. I've been so focused on this all week and working crazy long hours. It's nice to get out for a while and do something other than work."

"I'm sure you'll do great."

"Thanks for the vote of confidence. It helps, especially considering that Andrea is hoping that I fail." Hailey clearly remembered the evil gleam in Andrea's eye the entire time she was outlining Hailey's assignment.

"I hate to say this, Hailey, but you do need to watch your back with Andrea. I know for a fact that she purposely overloaded you for this job and assigned you technical aspects that she should be responsible for. I thought she would back off after it was clear you could handle the job, but it almost seems as if she's trying to sabotage you."

Before she could reply, Connor launched into the story of his first presentation with Grant's. Hailey tried to pay attention as he described the details of how he'd charmed all the high level executives, but she barely managed to smile and nod in the right places. She was completely distracted by the pretentious setting and specifically the lady sitting across from their table. The elegantly dressed, middle-aged woman kept shooting dirty looks their way, making Hailey feel very self-conscious. Was it that obvious that she didn't belong here? Hailey discreetly tried to check her hair and her simple blue dress. But her hair seemed to still be in place and there weren't any obvious stains or holes in her clothing. If Connor noticed the woman's disdain, he didn't say anything but seemed to blissfully continue the saga of his success.

Maybe the woman was just a snob or was in having an awful date. Hailey had just started imagining wild scenarios to account for the woman's behavior, when she suddenly realized Connor had asked her a question. But she didn't have a clue what he'd said.

Thankfully, she was saved from having to answer by the waiter bringing their food. Hailey appreciated that the service had been fast. Right now, she was just looking forward to being done with this place. It's not as if she didn't enjoy nice restaurants, but she just felt very conspicuous and awkward with this being their first date.

Even when the rude woman and her weary-looking date left the restaurant with one last parting glare in their direction, Hailey still didn't feel comfortable. Hailey's nicest dress was still nothing in comparison to the designer gowns worn by most of the other ladies. It was hard for Hailey to relax when she was deathly afraid of committing some faux pas like breaking a plate or spilling something on the pure white tablecloth. She knew it was supposed to be a romantic setting, complete with a candle at the center of their table. But Hailey was seriously trying to figure her chances of making it out of there without knocking the candle over and setting the whole place on fire.

Hailey carefully dissected the unidentifiable meat on her plate. It looked suspiciously like snails or maybe squid or octopus. She determinedly pierced a piece with her fork and popped it in her mouth.

Then she gagged.

It tasted awful, and the texture was even worse! She tried to cover her revulsion, continuing to smile and nod through Connor's tale of when he met the president. She resolutely swallowed.

Then she choked.

Unable to cover her coughing or tearing eyes, she grabbed for her water glass and knocked it over, thoroughly baptizing the white tablecloth. With the offensive meat still stuck in her throat, she grabbed for Connor's water and guzzled it down.

With her first good breath, she began apologizing.

Connor waved it off, saying simply that he was glad she was okay. The waiter came and wordlessly cleaned the table, replacing everything and then returning their plates of food to their original positions.

The worst part about the whole situation was that her plate of food had escaped the baptismal and waited patiently with high expectations of being eaten. But, no matter how much she tried to talk herself into it, she knew she wouldn't be able to swallow another bite.

At this point she would have given just about anything to be at a Dairy Queen.

Thankfully, Connor was thoroughly enjoying his own gourmet dinner and apparently didn't need her to participate in the conversation much. He launched into another story of how he almost crashed his plane. Though something had gone wrong mechanically, he'd been able to use his exceptional skill as a pilot to land the plane safely.

While he talked, Hailey found a compromise. She smiled, nodded, stuck the food in her mouth, chewed, and then unobtrusively spit it out into her napkin. Her technique required lots of water to flush the taste out of her mouth. The bread was actually very good, so by alternating bread with bites of her meal, she was able to adequately decrease the amount of food on her plate, and then rearrange the rest to appear as if she'd eaten.

When the waiter stopped by to refill her rapidly disappearing water for the third time, she sweetly asked for more napkins and even remarked on how good the bread was.

Eventually, Connor finished his food, and they left the French restaurant behind. All Hailey could think about was getting home so she could cry the whole experience out. She was definitely out of her league with Connor. Even with the coincidence of him being gone at the same time, there was no way he was her Santa.

"It's still so early, I'm not ready for the night to be over," Connor said as he pulled the Porsche back onto the street. "How about we go to this night club I know about? It's classy and fairly exclusive. There's dancing and we can talk and get to know each other a little more."

Hailey felt as if a boulder lodged itself in the pit of her stomach (or maybe it was that one piece of meat that she'd swallowed). She wasn't a nightclub type of girl. She might enjoy ballroom dancing if she ever had a chance to learn, but not nightclub dancing. She wasn't sophisticated. She wasn't trendy or modern. The truth was, she was boring. And she liked it that way.

"Okay," she found herself saying. Now why had she agreed to go somewhere she didn't want to go? Was she really just a spineless teenager that she couldn't disagree with the popular football star? She'd honestly been under the delusion that she had matured since then and grown at least some spine. She had stood up to Andrea in the interview, so why couldn't she state her opinion now?

Hailey morosely watched the passing lights, thoroughly disgusted with herself. Suddenly, her eyes picked up on a sign decorated with a multitude of beautiful Christmas lights.

She excitedly spoke up, "Connor, I have a better idea! Let's go to the Festival of Lights at the zoo!"

"W-what?" Connor stuttered, obviously surprised.

"Every year they decorate the zoo and botanical gardens with millions of Christmas lights. I haven't gone since I was a kid. Please, Connor! It'll be so much fun. I think we'll still have about an hour and a half before they close."

Connor suddenly smiled and replied, "Your wish is my command, m'lady."

Even with his sweet reply and the fact that he consented to go, Hailey got the impression that Connor still wasn't too pleased with the idea. But she didn't care that much. She did not want to go to a nightclub. She would have fun at the Festival even if Connor did nothing more than talk about himself the entire time.

Once at the zoo, Hailey popped out of the car like an excited five-year old. Grabbing Connor's hand without thought, she excitedly pulled him along with her to the entrance. She didn't want to waste any time.

An hour and a half might not be long enough to see everything. She'd read that they now decorated the zoo with approximately 2.5 million lights! It was sure to be breathtaking!

Connor paid their admission. As they walked through the entrance, Hailey practically squealed with delight. There was a huge tree that was at least thirty feet tall and decorated with thousands of LED lights.

"Isn't it beautiful?" Hailey exclaimed.

As they went past the tree, ahead of them was what the map called Swan Lake. Hailey watched in rapt fascination as a tall, fully be-decked, computer-controlled tree danced to Christmas music.

After watching for a solid ten minutes, Hailey became aware of Connor shifting impatiently. Connor held her hand as they moved on, and before long, he seemed to catch Hailey's excitement. He laughed with her as they watched the silly black light puppet show, oohed and aahed appropriately at the thousands upon thousands of lights in beautiful arrangements, and even seemed to appreciate seeing the animals in all their glory.

They laughed and talked as they rode the train through what seemed like a magical fantasy land. The myriad of lights created scenes that were almost unreal in their artistry. As Hailey watched Connor's eyes reflect the glow of the lights, she once again wondered whether he and Chris were the same man. Maybe he had just been as nervous as she was at dinner. He seemed completely different now. He seemed kinder and able to enjoy the simple things. He seemed more like Chris.

As the train came to a stop, Connor was describing the beautiful Christmas tree his family decorated every year. He seemed very close to his family, a fact Hailey found attractive. Likewise, Chris had mentioned his family several times. But there was something about Connor's manner that bothered her. What would normally be a sweet story about a family being together for Christmas, almost sounded like bragging from Connor's lips. In their previous conversations, Chris's manner of speaking had struck her as very humble, whereas Connor seemed to have a more arrogant tone.

But if Connor and Chris were the same man, maybe he was trying to appear different to throw her off track. She really wouldn't be surprised if that was the case. Both men seemed very intelligent. A trick like that wouldn't be difficult at all for him to pull off.

As they disembarked from the train, the loudspeaker started making an announcement about the Zoo closing soon. They hadn't made it through everything yet, and Hailey was disappointed to have it end so soon. There was so much to see and do; Hailey knew it was impossible to experience it all in such a short time. Maybe she could come back on another night. She might even be able to get tickets to one of the shows.

Hand-in-hand they started to make their way back to the entrance.

Connor paused. "Hailey, if you'll excuse me, I'm going to run to the restroom. How about I meet you over there?" He pointed ahead to where thousands of lights arched into a beautiful tunnel, almost like a rainbow that you could walk through.

Connor was gone awhile. She hoped he would make it back before the Zoo officially closed. As Hailey waited, she slowly walked back and forth beneath the tunnel. It really did feel like a fantasyland.

Midway beneath the canopy of lights, Connor suddenly appeared in front of her.

"We still have about ten minutes before they kick us out," he said. With a boyish smile, he handed her one of two covered Styrofoam cups. It's getting cold; I figured you might like something to warm up with before we leave.

How thoughtful! Hailey took a sip from the cup. Hot cocoa! As they sipped their cocoa, they talked about what their favorite part of the Festival had been.

Even as she talked with Connor, Hailey's mind was spinning. The more she'd thought about it, the more sure she was. Connor and Chris had to be the same man. They were the same tall height and had the same gorgeous blue eyes. Connor did seem very anxious to please her. Maybe the arrogance in his manner, along with the French restaurant and the ritzy nightclub, was simply a desire to impress her.

Another announcement came over the loudspeaker. "The Zoo will be closing in five minutes. Please make your way back to the main entrance."

By now, the tunnel was deserted. In fact, it seemed like they were the last lingering guests in the entire zoo. But Connor made no move to follow the instructions. Instead, he took Hailey's empty cup and set it down on the cement with his. He loosely held Hailey with his hands gently cupping her upper arms.

"Thank you, Hailey. I'm glad you wanted to come here. I've had a wonderful time with you tonight. I have one other thing for you—a souvenir of our first official date. Hailey hadn't noticed the small sack that had been at his feet. Opening it, he pulled out a small plush bear.

"I hope you like it," he said, his tone seeming unsure and hesitant for the first time.

Hailey accepted it, feeling laughter bubbling inside. The bear was wearing a Santa suit complete with the trademark Santa hat.

"Thank you, Connor. I love it." But she was really thanking him for more than the bear. She was thanking him for confirming what she'd already suspected. Connor was Chris.

Hailey was not the type to allow a man to kiss her on the first date. But this wasn't really her first date with him. This was the man who had talked with her and cared about her from the very first. He was the one who'd given her an ice skating lesson that had ended with them both flat on the ice. He was the one who gave up his free time to dress as Santa Claus and bring joy to children. This wasn't a stranger. This was her Santa, and he wanted to kiss her.

Connor wrapped his arms around her and pulled her close. She could have pulled away, but she didn't. Then his lips were on hers. She shyly returned his kiss. Her response seemed to give him confidence and his kiss lengthened, his lips moving over hers with increasing longing and a greater passion than Hailey was prepared for.

Her heart pounded.

Connor held her tightly, seeming to draw her even closer.

She couldn't breathe.

Suddenly, she broke the kiss and pushed him away.

CHAPTER 11

"I believe our newest staff member, Hailey Rhodes, has prepared a presentation for us."

Hailey tried to ignore the evil gleam of satisfaction in Andrea Holt's eyes. Hailey knew that Andrea fully expected her to fail.

Hailey gave herself a mental pep talk as she took her position at the front of the room. She was prepared. She was smart. She had good ideas. She could do this.

She tried to ignore that her entire body suddenly felt weak and shaky. *Keep it together!* she ordered herself. You cannot pass out! Turning to face her audience, she pasted a bright smile on her face and laced her fingers in front of her, trying to hide their tremors.

She immediately launched into her own short introduction, followed by her carefully rehearsed presentation. She tried to keep her tone steady and her expression relaxed, exactly as she had practiced in the mirror. As she talked, Hailey tried to make good eye contact with the faces lining the long conference table. Connor's was the only one that was remotely encouraging. Everyone else ranged from impassive, to openly skeptical, to Andrea's loosely-masked hostility.

Hailey tried to focus on her task and not the fact that there were some very high-level executives, including the CEO himself, listening and watching her every move. Her eyes scanned the fifteen people seated around the table, trying not to feel intimidated and self-conscious. As a whole, the group was much younger than she had anticipated. Grant's was a respected department store chain that had been in existence for over 100 years, yet there were only two executives who looked to be over fifty.

Hailey figured that she was probably still the youngest in the room, but that didn't intimidate her as much as the appearance of the executives did. The men were all dressed in expensive suits while the three women besides Hailey were dressed in what appeared to be expensive designer business attire that had been specially tailored to uniquely fit each woman. Dressed in a simple cornflower blue blouse and a black A-line skirt, Hailey felt frumpy to the point of embarrassment. The blouse had been one of her sister's castoffs, and the skirt was one that she'd gotten at a thrift store last week when she'd been desperate for appropriate clothes for work.

Despite her insecurities, Hailey warmed up and gained confidence as she talked. It helped having the Powerpoint presentation she had meticulously prepared. She didn't feel like the attention was focused on her as much when she was pointing out the data and other details of the slides.

Finally concluding her presentation with her suggestions for changes and improvements in her department, Hailey once again scanned every face around the table, trying to assess how they were reacting. Did they like her? Had she earned their respect? Did they agree with her suggestions or think she was way off base?

The CEO, Mr. Wright, wasn't even looking at her. His head was buried in something apparently far more interesting on his Ipad. Most of the other faces were impassive, but a few projected what might be a grudging look of respect. Then she saw Andrea's face. Pure hatred gleamed from her gray eyes. If she'd managed to make Andrea hate her even more, maybe that was a good sign.

Skimming past Andrea, Hailey's gaze stumbled over Connor's. His cocky grin said that he was proud and pleased with her. And then he slowly and deliberately winked. Hailey fought to keep herself from blushing, especially when he then raised one of his eyebrows and looked at her with a more intimate gaze than she felt comfortable with in a boardroom.

Memories of Saturday night and kissing him rushed over her. She'd pushed him and his passionate kisses away, making some lame excuse about how they needed to leave before they were kicked out. Connor had driven her home. She knew he was probably expecting a rousing sequel for their goodbye, but Hailey had jumped out of the car as soon as it had stopped. When he'd gotten out of the car as well, she'd thanked him profusely for the date and made it a quick parting. She'd even managed to have Connor's intended goodbye kiss be intercepted by her cheek. Then she'd turned and practically ran in to her sister's house.

"Are there any questions?" Hailey asked the audience, trying somewhat unsuccessfully to force her mind back to her current task.

She couldn't really put her finger on what had spooked her so much about Connor. She was still fully convinced that he was her Santa. But even so, Hailey had never been the type to kiss a man on the first date, especially not that kind of kiss. Maybe it had all been too fast. If Connor / Chris would just be honest about his identity, maybe she'd be able to accept his attentions more easily.

"I have a question, Miss Rhodes," Andrea said, her tone sharp and disapproving. Not waiting for a response, she continued. "Let me get this straight. You want us to discontinue a proven, quality brand that Grant's has carried for years and replace it with an unknown brand with no history. Exactly how does that make sense in your mind?"

Hailey tried to keep her anger under control. Was Andrea's rude and condescending manner as apparent to everyone else as it was to Hailey?

"Have you seen the products from the 'proven, quality brand,' Ms. Holt?" asked Hailey, looking the other woman directly in the eye and rising to the challenge. "They're ugly."

Hailey thought she heard a few actual giggles at her blunt statement, but she ignored them and continued. "Yes, Grant's has carried the brand for years, and yes, the clothes look like they've been carried for years. My mother might have found them stylish when she was a child, but I certainly wouldn't have worn them. And kids today probably wouldn't touch them with a ten foot stick."

Andrea opened her mouth, clearly intending to argue, but Hailey didn't give her a chance. With no pause, she continued. "We can't hold blindly to traditions when they no longer serve their function. You saw the sales reports. Sales aren't good, especially for that brand. I don't believe it's a matter of marketing; it's the brand itself. Plus, it doesn't help that these ugly clothes are overpriced. The new brand I am suggesting is very classically modern, if that makes sense. It's a new company that is producing well-made children's clothing that is simple and appealing to both children and their parents. And they are striving to make it affordable. So far, no nation-wide store has picked up this brand. I believe it would be to our advantage to be the major, if not sole, supplier.

Undeterred, Andrea pushed back again. "So you want us to just divorce the other company? Grant's is almost synonymous with their name at this point. Both of our companies have a good reputation for quality. We can't wager that on some upstart company."

"This isn't a dangerous gamble," Hailey explained. "Besides if you don't risk something sometime, you'll never go anywhere. The other company has obviously not made efforts to keep up with the children of today. Grant's has a great reputation with older people. But we now have a choice to either stay in the past and fizzle out, or earn a new reputation with this generation. Children today are going to be our customers for many tomorrows. If we aren't relevant in their eyes, we'll be just another 'old' store."

The room was silent. Andrea looked as if she wanted to say something but was for once speechless.

Finally, Mr. Wright cleared his throat. "Thank you, Miss Rhodes. The board will look over your report in detail, and we'll let you know our decision."

Hailey nodded and reclaimed her seat. The rest of the meeting passed in a quick blur. There were a few more matters that were discussed, but Hailey still had so much nervous adrenaline running through her that she couldn't focus. Instead, she replayed and analyzed her entire presentation, poking at the parts she could have explained better and generally making herself miserable.

It was lunchtime, and the meeting soon adjourned. Hailey retreated to her office. She had intended to work through lunch. The entire office was usually so much quieter when everyone was gone, and she had a mountain of work to do. She liked to use that time to work and take a quick minute to inhale some food on an afternoon break. But the adrenaline rush had left her weak, and after ten minutes of trying unsuccessfully to concentrate on her work, she decided to eat something now, hoping it would restart her brain.

People in this office seemed to consider their lunch break sacred, and the entire office was deserted. Hailey went to the employee break room where her lunch was waiting in a plastic container in the refrigerator. Since she didn't have money to afford daily lunch at a restaurant, she usually brought either a sandwich or dinner leftovers from the night before. And unless there was a special luncheon meeting, Hailey ate her lunch alone, which suited her just fine.

Hailey flipped one of the two light switches as she entered the dark room and let the door shut behind her. The lights lit on half the room. She really didn't need the harsh light of the fully lighted room. She was just going to warm her lasagna up in the microwave and take it to her desk to eat.

As she opened the refrigerator and bent to retrieve her lunch sack, she heard the door open behind her.

Turning, she saw Connor enter the room and come toward her.

"There you are, Hailey. I was looking for you."

"I was just getting my lunch," she said, holding her sack up as evidence. "I thought you'd be gone like everyone—"

Before she could finish her sentence, she was interrupted by Connor's lips on hers.

Hailey was so startled, she didn't even know how to react.

Connor pushed her against the wall, his body entrapping hers. Not able to even process what was happening, Hailey felt frozen, her fingers dumbly clinging to her lunch sack.

"You were so amazing in there," Connor said as he came up for air. "So smart . . . so sexy . . . and the way you handled Andrea . . ." He pressed his lips on hers again.

His fingers were in her hair. His mouth was moving passionately over her lips then down her neck. Apparently, her lack of response wasn't enough to faze him.

"Connor," Hailey said, finally managing to put her hands and the accompanying lunch sack between them. "I don't think this is the time or place. We're at work!"

"Everyone is gone," he replied, still trailing kisses along her neck. "I can't help it. Ever since Saturday night, all I can think about is kissing you. You're so beautiful."

He once again pressed his lips to hers, smothering her protests. She didn't want to hurt Connor, but she really didn't think the man she knew as Chris would act like this. She really did not want to be making-out in the break room!

She couldn't get out of his embrace because her back was at the wall. She pushed against his chest. He didn't budge. Even though she wasn't returning his affections, his kiss was becoming more passionate, more demanding.

Then, with sudden clarity, she knew. This was not Chris.

"Please stop, Connor!" Hailey said, craning her face away from him while wiggling and pushing his chest as hard as she could. If he wouldn't let her go, she was seriously considering kneeing him between the legs. "I really don't think—"

The break room door opened. Apparently hearing the sound, Connor finally let Hailey go abruptly and swung around. The CEO stood in the doorway.

CHAPTER 12

"Miss Rhodes, we will not be continuing your employment," Andrea Holt said, her tone brusque.

Hailey couldn't meet the woman's eyes. She couldn't handle seeing the look of evil satisfaction she knew would be on Andrea's face.

"I understand," Hailey replied quietly. She'd spent the last hour expecting this very thing. But that still didn't take away the embarrassment of the situation or the hurt of being fired.

After Mr. Wright had walked into the break room to find her involved in what must have seemed to be a heavy make-out session, Hailey had been overcome with humiliation, feeling her face immediately heat to crimson. Her first thought had been to defend herself with the opening line, 'This isn't what it looks like!' But then she realized how stupid that sounded. Even from Connor's perspective, it had been exactly what it looked like.

So she panicked. She had to get out of there fast.

Mumbling an "Excuse me," she bolted for the door, lunch sack still clutched in a death grip. She rushed past Mr. Wright, not even daring to make eye contact with either man.

She'd returned to her office and tried to work, but she really knew this meeting was inevitable. After an hour of misery, Andrea had called and asked to see her immediately. Now, being officially fired made Hailey's disgrace complete.

"We ask that you leave the building immediately," Andrea said, not seeming to bother trying to mask her enjoyment of the situation. "I'll have a security guard escort you to get your things."

Hailey stood and met Andrea's gaze one last time. Andrea's features were serene and almost expressionless, but her eyes were dancing. Not wanting to spend another moment in the room with the woman, Hailey turned to quickly leave quietly.

With her hand on the doorknob, she paused, hit with a bolt of sudden, intense anger. She should not be slinking out of here like a dog with his tail between his legs! She had done nothing wrong! She'd been trying to get Connor to stop. So why was she letting Andrea win?

"I would like to speak with Mr. Wright before I go," she said, turning back to face Andrea. She already knew it would do no good to try to explain what had happened to Andrea. Her boss had already been looking for a reason to fire her. There was no way Andrea would listen or be understanding when the situation was enabling her to do what she'd already been wanting. Hailey suddenly didn't want to give up without a fight, and the best way to clear her name would be to go over Andrea's head and do what she should have done immediately.

"Mr. Wright is not here," Andrea replied, dashing Hailey's sudden hope. "He was finishing some last minute details here in the office before he had to catch a flight. He explained the situation to me and asked that I inform you in his absence."

There was silence. Hailey and Andrea glared at each other as strong emotions made the air between them tense and thick.

"I would like the chance to defend myself," Hailey gritted out. "The scene Mr. Wright walked in on really wasn't as it seemed."

"You have no defense, Miss Rhodes. You were only hired a few weeks ago. Employees on probation can be let go for any reason at any time. And your little lunchtime recreation gave us plenty of reason."

Hailey felt a wave of helplessness wash over her. There was nothing she could do. She had been found guilty and sentenced without a trial.

"What about Mr. Montgomery?" Hailey couldn't resist asking. She wondered if he was facing a similar fate. Although he had been the instigator, Hailey would still feel bad if his actions with her had ruined his career. "Is his employment being terminated as well?"

"Not that it's any of your business," Andrea replied, "but no. Connor Montgomery has been with Grant's for several years with a proven track record. Unlike you, he is not a recent hire and on probation. Mr. Wright has instructed me to write a letter of reprimand and place it in his file."

Hailey knew that Andrea would have normally withheld the information on Connor's consequences just to be spiteful, but the fact that their punishments were so vastly different had probably been too much to resist the opportunity to rub it in. It wasn't fair. She needed this job. She had done great work these past few weeks, and it was maddening to have it all be wiped away because of something that hadn't even been her fault.

She wanted to plead her case and explain what had really happened. But the wicked gleam of triumph in Andrea's eyes let Hailey know that her petitions would fall on deaf ears. Hailey had lost.

"I think the security guard is waiting to escort you, Miss Rhodes. I believe our conversation is over. You may go now."

Hailey felt her face heat up at Andrea's condescending tone. For the first time, she felt tears burning behind her eyes. Without another word, she left the room in complete humiliation.

It took Hailey about thirty seconds to gather her few personal belongings from her office. As she walked beside Eddie, the security guard, to the elevator, she made no eye contact with any of the other employees and struggled to swallow down the tears. Office gossip was very efficient, and by now, everyone probably knew she'd been fired and also knew the reason. Hailey felt as if they were all staring at her, judging what she had done and secretly laughing at her consequences. Whether the others' reactions were real or imagined didn't really matter. For Hailey, it truly was a walk of shame.

Eddie's walkie-talkie began squawking as soon as they reached the elevator.

"I think you can find your way out from here," Eddie said. "My boss wants me to check some equipment on this floor."

The elevator dinged its arrival and opened. Hailey managed to mumble a 'thank you' and entered the elevator. She pushed the button for the underground parking garage. The door started to close. Hailey bit her lip, trying to keep the tears from spilling over until after she made it to her car. The door was almost closed when someone apparently pushed the down button again. It suddenly switched direction and reopened.

Connor Montgomery appeared at the door. Seeing Hailey, his face registered surprise, and he paused as if unsure. Then, as if putting a mask on, Connor's features drained of expression. He boarded the elevator and turned to face the front as the door finally slid shut.

Hailey couldn't handle the strained silence. "They fired me."

No response.

"At least they didn't fire you. Andrea said you're just getting a letter of reprimand."

Still no response.

"On the bright side, I guess us dating won't be an issue now!" she said with a slightly hysterical giggle. What was she saying? She didn't even know that she would ever go out with Connor again after his behavior, but she wasn't thinking straight. She felt as if she didn't even know which end was up, and now with the addition of Connor's strange silence, she found herself babbling.

Connor continued to stare straight ahead, his features expressionless, as if she'd never said anything. More than that, he was acting as if he didn't even see her, as if she didn't exist. Was he angry with her? She hadn't done anything wrong. She hadn't wanted him to kiss her in the employee break room. So then, why was she now feeling so guilty, as if the entire messy situation was her fault?

She opened her mouth to apologize for getting him in trouble, but caught herself and stopped. She wasn't going to apologize to him! He'd gotten himself in trouble!

The elevator dinged their arrival on the underground level. Connor wordlessly exited the elevator in front of her. He didn't once glance back at her.

Connor had accosted her with his unwanted attentions, got her fired, and now rudely snubbed her. She should be furious with him after everything that had happened. But all she could feel was the sting of his obvious rejection.

Hailey's breath came in short gasps as sobs caught in her throat and began to overwhelm her. She somehow managed to make it to her car even with her vision blurred from tears. As she opened her driver's side door, Connor zoomed past in his Porsche, clearly exceeding the 5 mile per hour speed limit.

Hailey enclosed herself in her car, leaned her head against the steering wheel, and let the sobs overtake her. And the worst part was knowing she would have to confess to both Jamie and the real Chris as to how and why she had been fired.

CHAPTER 13

"Why didn't you hit him?" Jamie demanded, clearly exasperated.

"I was going to!" Hailey replied. "But it all happened so fast. I told him to stop, but before I could do anything else, the CEO was standing in the doorway!"

Hailey had been sitting on a barstool at the breakfast bar in the kitchen and surfing the internet for jobs when Jamie had gotten home from work. Hailey had wasted no time in telling Jamie the story of being fired, and Jamie had wasted no time in hitting the roof.

"Hailey, I could have told you Connor Montgomery was a cad! He was that way in high school too!"

"I didn't know! He wasn't in my class; he was in yours. I just always saw him as the unattainable popular guy every girl wanted to date. Then when we were both working for Grant's and he asked me out . . . I was flattered."

Hailey had known Jamie would be upset with the news Hailey had been fired. She'd thought Jamie would be quiet, depressed, worried, and maybe even spend the evening brooding alone in her room. What she hadn't counted on was Jamie's anger, especially not the anger toward Hailey herself.

Hailey hadn't seen her sister this animated in a long time. Jamie's eyes were flashing and her arms flailing in grand gestures to match her words. She wasn't just mad. She was livid.

"You didn't even tell me you went out with him! I would have told you he was no good!"

"Jamie, you've been so stressed and busy that I didn't think you cared about my social life."

Jamie shot right back. "You're usually so level-headed and smart that I wouldn't think you'd need your big sister to tell you that a guy is a jerk! But you kissed him on your date—on your first date. With that kind of encouragement, he probably thought you were the type of girl who wouldn't mind a little tryst in the break room!"

"I only kissed him because I thought he was Chris!" Hailey hiccupped, bit her trembling lip, and wiped at the tears that had begun flowing again. She'd thought she had cried all the tears out in the car, but Jamie's harsh reaction had triggered reserves Hailey didn't know she had.

Apparently seeing her sister's distress, Jamie sighed heavily and took a seat on the barstool beside her. Hailey had told Jamie all about Chris. Much to Hailey's surprise, her usually skeptical sister had found the whole situation very romantic, saying that any young guy who took off work to play Santa every year had to be a good one.

"I know you didn't instigate it, Hailey. It isn't fair that you got fired and he didn't, especially for a situation you didn't want to be involved in. But it's also true that you didn't exactly use good judgment. Now you don't have a job, we still have rent to pay, and you have to explain to Chris why you got fired for making-out with another guy."

"I'll come up with the money for the rent, Jamie. I told you I would, and I still intend to pay it. I know we've had some extra expenses since we had to replace the refrigerator, but I may still have enough money with the pay I've already earned. We don't get charged a late fee until after the 22nd. I'll have the money before then."

Their arrangement was that Hailey covered the cost of rent while Jamie covered utilities, food, and everything else. Jamie didn't make much money in her job as a receptionist at a medical clinic, but they each had still managed to pool their resources to cover the bills every month, even after Hailey lost her teaching job. But between Christmas and the broken refrigerator, Hailey already knew Jamie had nothing left to contribute to the rent. Though she didn't want Jamie to know, Hailey was really scared she wouldn't have enough.

Jamie sighed. "Well, maybe you can do some substituting until you find something else, but there's no way you'll get paid in time to help us this month."

"Substituting is so irregular; it's hard to count on any income from it. I'm trying to look at job openings, but I don't even know which direction to take. The maddening thing about losing the job at Grant's is that I was good at it! I was learning everything really fast, and I think I did really well on my presentation this morning. I haven't had much luck with teaching; maybe I should change careers. I probably won't ever get an opportunity like the one I had at Grant's though. Don't worry; I'll find something even if I have to scrub toilets, though I'm sure I'd be pretty lousy at that one."

Jamie let out an exasperated breath. "What is it you want to do, Hailey? Do you want to teach, be a buyer for a department store, or do something else entirely? You're smart and determined. You're always going to be good at whatever you try to do. But you need to do what God is calling you to do. What gives you joy and fulfills you?"

Hailey was silent, thinking. Deep down, she knew the answers to Jamie's questions. She may have been distracted and even enamored with the thought of being a high level business executive, but she loved being a teacher. What she'd liked most in her short job as a buyer was getting to choose products for kids. She liked kids. She really could think of nothing more fulfilling than getting to teach them every day.

At Hailey's silence, Jamie continued, her voice softening and her eyes locking suspiciously bright. "Hailey, I know you've made a lot of sacrifices for me and my family—a lot more than I'm comfortable with. But I don't want you to give up what you love for me as well. I want you to be happy. I won't always need your help. Someday I want to be able to stand on my own two feet, and at that point, I hope I haven't screwed up your life too much. Do what you want to do, Hailey. No cleaning toilets for my sake. If you're doing what God has called you to do, He'll take care of the rest, including our rent."

Hailey had gotten discouraged when she lost her job teaching first grade, but maybe Jamie was right. Maybe God still had a plan for her to do what she loved; she just needed to be patient.

For the first time in a long while, Hailey had caught a glimpse of hope for Jamie. Her sister had been so discouraged and depressed for so long, Hailey had begun to wonder if Jamie would ever recover from her divorce. But tonight, she had seen Jamie's anger that, although uncomfortably directed at Hailey, had been more encouraging to see than her usual mask of apathy. Now she was seeing a glimpse of Jamie's faith. Hailey had been praying for Jamie for so long, and to now see that Jamie's faith had not been a casualty almost made her want to cry the good kind of tears!

Jamie stood and stretched. "I have to go make sure Spencer is doing his homework, and then I'll get the kids some supper. I think it's a soup and sandwiches night."

As Jamie left, the positive feelings left with her, and Hailey sat blindly staring at the computer screen. Her mind went back to brooding over the events of the day. She was still shocked that Jamie had been so mad at her.

With sudden painful clarity, Hailey realized the truth. Jamie was right. Hailey had used bad judgment. She hadn't even liked Connor on their date, but she'd made excuses for him, wanting him to be Chris.

Before, she hadn't understood why all kinds of bad things had happened to her when she hadn't done anything wrong. But this one was her fault. She'd had many opportunities to prevent it from happening, but she hadn't. She could have asked Connor outright if he was Chris. She could have been more adamant in resisting Connor when he first made advances in the break room. She could have hit him, kicked him, anything to make sure he got the message loud and clear. She also could have stayed around and explained the situation to Mr. Wright instead of running off like she was guilty.

What if that job had been God's will for her and she'd screwed it up? Suddenly it was as if she was looking back on her life with a different kind of lens. She had been almost angry with God because of all the bad circumstances she felt she hadn't deserved. But maybe she did deserve them. She was always messing up in some way by making stupid decisions or committing small sins that she didn't really even like to acknowledge as sins. In fact, she probably deserved much worse than she got! Thank the Lord she didn't always get what she deserved!

Her cell phone rang. She looked at the display. It was Chris. She had given him her cell number weeks ago so he could call her on his business trip any time he had a spare moment. She silently prayed Chris would be understanding, took a deep breath, and answered it.

"Hi, Chris."

"Hi, Hailey! How are you?"

His voice sounded so cheerful! She hated to tell him what had happened, especially since he might end up hating her by the time she finished this conversation.

"I got fired from Grant's," she said, opting for the blunt approach.

"Oh, no! What happened?"

So Hailey told him the whole story, sparing no detail. She tried to be brutally honest about her own actions, even outlining the date she'd had with Connor and their kiss. She finished with telling how Connor hadn't even acknowledged her presence in the elevator.

There was silence on the line.

"Chris, are you there?"

"Yes, I'm here," he replied. "I heard. I'm a little shocked that you went out with the guy in the first place and then kissed him. I'm honestly just trying to figure out what to say."

He was mad! Now she'd ruined everything, and he wouldn't even want to take her to the Christmas party!

"I'm so sorry, Chris! I only kissed him because I thought he was you!"

"What?"

She felt herself blushing like he was right there in the room gawking at her. How could she admit that she had feelings for him, especially since she didn't even know who he was or what he looked like?

"I thought he was you," she repeated. "He's has the same height and body type as you. He has blue eyes and dark hair. And he liked me! He got me the job as a buyer even though others didn't want to hire me. At times he was very sweet and said or did things that reminded me of you. I thought it was too much of a coincidence. You've been so secretive; I didn't know what to think. I didn't know why you were playing this game, but I decided to go ahead and play along. When I kissed him, I thought I was kissing you. Obviously I was wrong, and you have no idea how sorry I am."

"Hailey, are you there? . . . I might be losing you . . . going . . . tunnel . . . not kidding—"

"Chris, are you there? Chris, don't do this to me!"

Hailey heard a few more parts of words. She thought he said something about bad timing, but she wasn't sure. Then the line went completely dead.

Hailey put the phone on the counter and stared at it, waiting. He was going to call back any minute, as soon as he was out of the tunnel. He wouldn't lie about something like that. He'd obviously been upset. But he wouldn't lie, would he?

The seconds ticked by. She'd just put her heart out there, confessing her feelings and saying that she'd wanted to kiss him. Did that make a difference to him? Would he even care?

The phone remained silent. After a full five minutes, Hailey could feel the tears coming yet again.

The phone rang.

She snatched it up, not even glancing at the number.

"Hello?"

"Miss Rhodes? This is Andrea Holt."

CHAPTER 14

I don't want to be here! Hailey thought as she followed the security guard back through the hallways.

If she could have come up with any way to avoid coming back to the Grant's office, she would have. Her only consolation was that she had managed to put it off until the last minute. Andrea would be panicking that she wasn't going to show up. The thought of Andrea panicking gave Hailey more satisfaction than she would be willing to admit.

Andrea had called last night wanting to know where Hailey's presentation and the supporting documents were. Hailey had told her where to find them in her former office, but Andrea said the memory stick wasn't where it was supposed to be. Hailey honestly didn't know where it was, but Andrea had rather rudely insisted Hailey come back in to the office tomorrow to find the memory stick and hand it over with the rest of her files. Hailey wanted to flatly refuse, but Andrea had also said that Hailey's final check should be ready for her to pick up.

Andrea had made the mistake of mentioning that she needed Hailey's presentation material for a meeting in the afternoon. So Hailey had waited until the last minute to show up. The fact that it was lunchtime and all of the employees were gone was added incentive. Hailey really didn't want to face any questions or knowing glances. Of course, since she was no longer an employee, she had the privilege of being escorted by Eddie, the same burly security guard who escorted her almost twenty-four hours ago.

Eddie unlocked the door to her former office. Hailey quickly found the file Andrea wanted, but couldn't find the memory stick that held her presentation. It had also been saved to her computer, but she was sure they had probably already changed her password denying her access. Then she remembered. She had used the memory stick for her presentation in the conference room yesterday. It was probably still plugged into the computer where she'd left it.

Hailey explained the situation to Eddie, and he followed her to the conference room. Since nothing important was stored in the conference room, it was never locked.

Hailey opened the door and reached to the right to flip the light switch. Light flooded the room, and two figures scrambled up from the conference table. Shock raced through Hailey like electricity as Connor Montgomery and Andrea Holt frantically tried to button their shirts.

Tense silence filled the room, and Hailey suddenly wanted to laugh. As Jamie had put it, Connor was a cad. He obviously hadn't learned his lesson yesterday. But he had apparently found a much more willing partner for a lunchtime rendezvous.

Holding in her laughter, Hailey waited several long seconds, purposely prolonging the tension. Then she delicately cleared her throat and said seriously, "I see you're petitioning Ms. Holt to write a nice letter of reprimand, Connor."

Connor glared at Hailey, and Andrea had the decency to blush while continuing to fumble with her blouse.

Hailey casually walked over to the computer and removed the memory stick. She then placed both the file and the stick on the conference table.

"Here are the things you asked for, Andrea," she said sweetly. "I'm sure you'll need them after Connor has finished presenting his case."

At the couple's continued silence, Hailey smiled and walked to where Eddie was waiting at the open door. Turning one last time, she said, "Oh, and this is just a suggestion, but next time you might want to choose one of the locked offices for your lunchtime recreation."

With one last friendly smile, Hailey flipped the light switch, returning the conference room and its residents to darkness. She then firmly shut the door behind her.

As they walked back to the elevator, Eddie couldn't hide his chuckles of amusement. "That was beautifully played, Miss Rhodes."

Hailey smiled and shook her head. "All the offices that can be locked, and they choose the one room that can't be? For Pete's sake, they each have their own locking offices and keys to probably a dozen more!"

Eddie shook his head, white teeth flashing against his dark skin. "I would guess the element of danger is part of the appeal, at least for Mr. Montgomery. Since you no longer work here, Miss Rhodes, I don't mind telling you that both the security guards and maintenance crew are very careful to always knock before entering a dark room. We've seen more with our eyes and our cameras' eyes than we ever wanted to."

Following the direction of his discreet nod, Hailey saw a security camera in the corner by the elevator.

Eddie continued. "Let's just say, this isn't the first time I've seen evidence of those two being involved. Of course, I've also seen evidence of Mr. Montgomery trying to get involved with just about every woman in the building."

Hailey felt a strange mixture of disgust and relief. She was appalled at Connor's blatant womanizing, especially in the work place, but she was also relieved that she had escaped involvement with him. She saw now that he was nothing like her Chris. Of course, Chris had never called her back last night after claiming to lose reception in a 'tunnel.' So, maybe she was wrong about his character too. She didn't exactly have a good track record at this point.

Eddie escorted Hailey down a couple floors to the human resources department where she picked up her check. Then he stayed with her until the elevator opened into the parking garage.

"Thanks, Eddie," Hailey said in parting.

"No, thank you for the entertainment, Miss Rhodes!"

When Hailey got to her car, she looked at her paycheck. She knew how much was already in her account, and she knew how much she needed to pay for rent. Their landlady, Mrs. Whipple was an older widowed woman who looked like someone's sweet little grandma. But she acted more like a demanding general. She was not very nice or understanding, and Hailey had a very real fear that they would be kicked out if they missed even one payment. She already had her suspicions that Mrs. Whipple would really like to see them leave so she could raise the rent for new unsuspecting tenants.

Hailey would head straight to the bank to deposit the check, but she couldn't wait to find the balance then. She did the mental math. Then she did it again. Dread settled like a boulder in the pit of her stomach. She didn't have enough.

CHAPTER 15

Hailey knocked on the door and waited. She hid her shaking hands in her coat pockets and practiced a friendly smile. It was the morning of December 22nd. The rent was due, and she didn't have the money to pay it.

The door opened a crack, just enough for Hailey to see one bright eye and a bit of gray hair.

"Hi, Mrs. Whipple. It's Hailey Rhodes. I was wondering if I might have a word with you?"

"Of course," she replied, opening the door wide. "But I have to leave soon for BINGO down at the senior center."

"This won't take long." Hailey could have just called and spoken to Mrs. Whipple over the phone, but she hoped the landlady would be more understanding if Hailey made her petition in person.

Hailey looked around Mrs. Whipple's immaculate house as she followed the woman's heavily perfumed trail through the entryway and into the living room. Jamie's family had been renting the house before Steve left and Hailey had moved in, so Hailey had never before had reason to come to Mrs. Whipple's residence. She had previously just mailed the rent check.

Hailey had met Mrs. Whipple a few times when she'd come to the rental. The elderly lady had always been dressed to the nines. She wore bright colors complete with every matching accessory imaginable. Everything from her purse to her earrings was coordinated, the effect being attractive but bordering on gaudy. With her purple and teal ensemble complete with earrings that sounded like little chimes when she walked, Hailey saw that today was no different.

Mrs. Whipple gestured for Hailey to sit on the couch while she took the chair opposite. As Hailey moved to sit, she saw two cats perched on the couch, right where she was supposed to sit. What should she do? Should she move one of the cats over? She glanced back to see Mrs. Whipple gently pick up a third cat who'd been sitting on her chair. She sat down with the cat gently cradled in her lap.

Hailey looked at the calico cat in her way. The cat looked at Hailey as if he was a king and Hailey merely a pesky serf. Hailey hesitantly touched the cat, trying to gently scoot him over.

The cat growled.

Hailey jerked her hand back. What should she do? She reached both hands down to carefully pick the cat up as she'd seen Mrs. Whipple do. The cat growled again, this time louder.

"Oh, stop that, Oscar," Mrs. Whipple said mildly. "Pay him no mind, Miss Rhodes. He's harmless. He thinks he owns the place. Just move him aside."

Determined, Hailey quickly scooted Oscar over next to the other one, while the cat's growls increased to a loud whining howl.

Finally able to sit, Hailey tried to ignore the cat glaring evilly beside her.

"Now what can I do for you, Miss Rhodes?" Mrs. Whipple asked pleasantly.

Why was she being so nice? In every other encounter Hailey had experienced with the landlady, the elderly lady had been brusque to the point of being rude. Why was today so different? Hailey was suddenly very suspicious.

She was even more unnerved when she looked around the room and saw even more eyes staring at her. Mrs. Whipple didn't have just three cats. On almost every piece of furniture was perched a cat. There were at least ten that Hailey could see, and they were all staring at Hailey. As a general rule, Hailey didn't mind cats, but she did mind them in large quantities. Her only consolation was that the cats and the entire house appeared very clean and well cared for. With such an audience, though, Hailey wanted to get this errand done as quickly as possible.

"I brought you a check for our rent, Mrs. Whipple, but unfortunately, it isn't for the entire amount. I lost my job, and my sister and I are short on money right now. I'm sure we'll be able to make up the difference in the check next month."

"No, that won't be necessary," Mrs. Whipple replied. "When I didn't receive a check or hear from you at the usual time, I assumed you knew."

"Knew what?" Hailey asked, unable to mask the fear and panic caused by Mrs. Whipple's words. Was she kicking them out?

In an apparent psychotic mood swing, the calico cat cuddled up against her leg and looked up at her as if seeking affection.

"Your rent has already been paid."

"It's already been paid? What do you mean? How is that possible?" Had Jamie found a way to pay and not mentioned it?

"A man called me and said he'd like to pay your rent," Mrs. Whipple explained. "I didn't see a problem with it. I knew you'd been having some issues with employment. He sent a check the next day."

"Who was it?" Hailey demanded, her pride feeling the sting of accepting charity. "I have to pay him back. I can't let someone pay our rent for an entire month!"

"Miss Rhodes, he didn't pay for a month. He paid for six!"

Tears started welling up in Hailey's eyes. Who would do such a thing? She had been so worried about making that rent payment, and now it had been paid for her.

As her mind whirled with possibilities, she absently began to pet the ball of fur beside her. The cat leaned into her touch, arching his back as her hand slid across his sleek fur.

As far as she knew, Jamie was the only one who knew of their financial situation. Who would care enough to find out and take care of her biggest concern?

Then she knew. Chris. He had called her back the next day after supposedly losing reception in a tunnel. But they hadn't talked long even then. He'd been away on business and claimed to be extremely busy, but Hailey suspected he was still upset with her. Jamie had mentioned one other time that Chris had called to talk when she'd been gone. But if he had really wanted to talk to her, he could have called on her cell phone.

"Are you okay, dear?" Mrs. Whipple asked gently.

Hailey nodded. "I'm just surprised, and I don't really understand."

The crazy cat began to purr.

"He seemed like a very nice gentleman. I assumed he was one of your friends. When I didn't hear from you right away, I thought he'd probably decided to tell you himself."

Composing herself, Hailey asked, "Mrs. Whipple, what was the name on the check?"

The older lady smiled a bit mischievously. "He requested that I not tell you if you asked. I think he's probably one of your friends, but he wants to remain anonymous. He told me to just tell you it was a gift from Santa."

CHAPTER 16

"Are you shopping, James?" Hailey asked with pure orneriness. "I didn't know you were in the market."

Since they were young, Hailey had teased her sister with the nickname James, but Jamie had been having such a difficult time lately, Hailey had unconsciously stopped using the name. Now, seeing Jamie with a magazine sporting a picture of a handsome dark-haired man along with the headline, 'Hottest Bachelors in Cincinnati,' Hailey couldn't resist poking fun.

Though Jamie tried to shrug nonchalantly, she blushed like a teenager and threw the magazine on the coffee table. "The first time I got married, I did it for love. Since that worked out so well for me, I figured the second time I should try to marry for money."

"And that magazine has some good candidates?" Hailey asked.

"They definitely have very good resumes," Jamie replied.

Hailey had left Mrs. Whipple's house feeling as if a huge weight had been lifted off her shoulders. Though she hated the thought of Chris paying her rent, she was also very relieved to have the problem solved. She would find a way to pay Chris back, but it was so nice to have the pressure relieved if just for a little while.

On her way to the store after Mrs. Whipple's, Hailey had answered a call on her cell phone. It had been that private school Chris had said needed a teacher. Hailey had emailed her resume to Chris's sister, but she really hadn't thought anything would come of it. But the principal himself had called her, requesting that she come to the school immediately for an interview. Though not dressed or prepared for an interview, Hailey had seized the opportunity. The interview had gone well, and the principal had said they would be making their decision and calling her very soon. Apparently, they wanted to fill the position as soon as possible so the new teacher could start right after New Year's Day. The principal had interviewed other candidates but had decided to interview Hailey as well after running across her resume in his inbox at the last minute.

Hailey had no idea if she would get the job, and as excited as she was, she didn't want to tell Jamie about the interview until she knew the results. She didn't want Jamie getting her hopes up only to have them dashed. Dealing with Hailey's own dashed hopes would be difficult enough.

Overall, it had been a wonderful day, and now, it was an added bonus to walk into the living room to find Jamie perusing a magazine filled with hot guys. Maybe this was yet another small sign that Jamie was moving on from her heartbreak over Steve.

Hailey flopped down on the couch next to Jamie. She could hear the kids outside playing in the snow. From the sound of it, Shaya was trying to direct her two siblings to make a snowman, but they weren't cooperating.

"Where were you?" Jamie asked. "I tried to call to remind you to get milk, but you didn't answer."

"I remembered the milk," Hailey replied. She then added simply, "I had to take care of the rent and run some other errands."

Hailey had thought about telling Jamie about Chris paying their rent for the next six months, but she wasn't sure how Jamie would react. It was definitely possible that Jamie would be very upset, stressed, and insist on working herself to death to pay the money back as soon as possible. So Hailey had decided to wait before she mentioned anything about it to Jamie, at least until she had talked to Chris.

"I had my cell with me, though," Hailey said, taking her phone out of her purse. "I didn't think I'd missed a call." She checked the call history. "No, it's not saying I missed anything."

"Your phone is screwed up," Jamie concluded. "Maybe you've dropped it too much. You probably need to take it to the store to have them look at it."

"Like I have money for that. But at least that might explain why I haven't heard from Chris much. Maybe his calls aren't coming through."

"Did everything go alright with Mrs. Whipple?" Jamie asked.

"Everything is taken care of," Hailey replied cheerfully. "I was lucky to escape her psychotic cat, but other than that, everything went fine."

Trying to distract Jamie from asking more questions, Hailey told the story of Mrs. Whipple's mentally disturbed cat. With a grimace, Hailey recalled how, after petting the purring cat, she had gotten up to leave. As she had looked down at her new friend, the cat had looked up with his eerie green eyes and hissed at her.

Hailey was a little afraid Jamie would want more details of the visit with Mrs. Whipple. Jamie would know Hailey didn't usually hand-deliver the check. But either Jamie was willing to take Hailey's word for it, or she just didn't want to know.

The kids came in from outside covered in snow, effectively ending any further conversation. Jamie sprang into action to clean them up, and Hailey followed to help.

All through dinner and loads of laundry, Hailey kept waiting for Chris to call. Finally, the kids were in bed, and she couldn't take it any longer. She was going to call him. He'd always been the one to call her before; she had never called him. But after discovering today that he'd paid her rent, she decided she couldn't wait any longer.

She found his number on her phone and, before she could change her mind, pressed 'send.' It rang once and was answered.

"No one is available to take your call. Please leave a—"

Hailey hung up.

It was maddening that not even his cell phone message gave any clues about his true identity. She'd obviously been wrong about Connor being Chris, but could Chris be someone else in her life? It would make sense that he knew either her or Jamie. How else would he know that they needed help with their rent? Maybe she could ask Jamie if she had mentioned their situation to anyone. Hailey recalled briefly discussing their rent with Chris the night of the Downtown Dazzle, but she'd been vague and hadn't in any way suggested they would need help. Chris had to have gotten details from somewhere.

As Hailey got ready for bed, her mind mulled over the possibilities, finally hitting on an idea. Maybe her old boss, Jerry, was Chris! Sure, she'd always thought Jerry was older than early thirties; but maybe Chris had stretched the truth a little or Jerry was younger than he appeared. It made sense in a bizarre sort of way. Jerry hadn't been there in the office when Hailey had first arrived. He could have easily changed out of the Santa suit and slipped in while Hailey was in the restroom. Jerry had always been nice to her. It was Jerry who had helped her get the job as a buyer. He would have known she was short on money after losing her job for a third time. Maybe she was just grabbing at straws but maybe, just maybe . . .

Hailey fell asleep with her brain chasing circles with different scenarios, finally concluding that Jerry had to be Chris. The problem was that Hailey wasn't remotely attracted to Jerry. After a month of anticipating, finding out that Jerry was her Secret Santa would be extremely disappointing.

Hailey woke the next morning with an image in her head. It was the memory of dark waves of hair escaping from under a Santa hat that had been knocked askew. And then she knew she'd been wrong last night. Jerry wasn't Chris. When they had fallen at the ice skating rink, Hailey had seen Chris's thick, dark hair right before he'd put the hat back in place. In contrast, Jerry's best hair days were a thing of the past. The head of hair she'd seen at the skating rink was clearly not that of a balding man. So, unless Chris had been wearing a fabulous toupee under the Santa Claus hat and wig, Hailey could rest assured that Jerry was not her Santa Claus.

Hailey found Jamie making pancakes in the kitchen. It was December 23. Their parents were going to be spending Christmas with their brother this year, so Jamie, Hailey, and the kids were on their own for the festivities. Hailey was determined to do the most with what they had and try to make Christmas as special as she could for her sister, nephew, and nieces.

Jamie had taken the day off so she could do some last minute shopping with whatever money they could scrape together. She and Jamie didn't have much to spend on gifts, but she hoped the kids would appreciate the few things they were able to get. Hailey didn't feel like she could spend the money she had intended for rent. After all, she still intended to pay Chris back. Maybe she could make it up to the kids when she got a new job.

Hailey was planning to stay with the kids while Jamie shopped. Then tonight was when she finally made good on the bet she'd lost a month ago. Her heart accelerated at the thought of the Christmas party with Chris.

With the kids seated at the breakfast bar, Hailey joined in with the fun. In the middle of their laughter over yet another one of Jamie's pitifully-shaped pancakes, the doorbell rang.

Curious about the unusual possibility of a morning visitor, everyone went to the door. Hailey looked through the keyhole and then opened the door. A UPS man stood there with his arms loaded down with boxes.

"Hailey Rhodes? Santa sent you some packages!"

CHAPTER 17

The packages were set in the living room by the Christmas tree. The UPS man was gone before Hailey could even question him, and the packages were quickly opened. Brightly colored gifts emerged from the boxes. Each gift was labeled with a name. Hailey watched in stunned silence as each child opened their gifts. New winter coats, games, and books soon littered the floor. Shaya was delighted with a large art kit. Sylvie squealed with pure joy with her first look at her beautiful new baby doll.

A simple envelope with Spencer's name on it lay at the bottom of one of the boxes. Jamie handed it to Spencer. As he read the note inside, his eyes grew round in shock.

"Mom, it's . . . BASEBALL!"

Jamie and Hailey crowded around Spencer, reading over his shoulder as he clutched the paper in his trembling hand. The note stated simply that Spencer was enrolled in a baseball academy complete with an indoor league. His tuition had been paid for the next six months. It involved Saturday and two evenings every week, and he was to start immediately after New Year's.

At Spencer's gift, Hailey's heart filled up to the brim where it overflowed in tears streaming down her face.

Jamie looked up at Hailey, smiling and waving her own gift. "It's a gift card so I can buy some new clothes!"

Completely overwhelmed, Hailey plopped on the floor, right in the middle of the ripped wrapping paper, empty boxes, new clothes, and exciting toys.

"Hailey, who did this?" Jamie asked. "It was your name on the outside of all of the boxes. Who sent us all this?"

Without a doubt, Hailey knew the answer to Jamie's question.

"It was Chris!" she choked out through her tears.

What she didn't know was how or why he'd done it.

"Open your present, Hailey," Jamie said nodding to the wrapped box beside Hailey. "Let's see what he got you."

Dazed, Hailey slowly unwrapped the gift. Lifting the lid on the box, she found a beautiful red dress nestled in the tissue paper.

Jamie squealed. "It's beautiful! He got it for you to wear for the party tonight!"

Hailey gently lifted the dress, the silky folds unfolding to reveal a stunning evening gown. Hailey glanced at the tag. It was her size.

"How did he know?" she asked, feeling confused and overwhelmed. How did he know that I didn't have a dress. And how did he know my size?"

Jamie suddenly looked away and began busily picking up the mess of boxes and wrapping paper. The kids were enthralled with their new things and paying no attention to the adults.

"Jamie?" Hailey asked suspiciously.

Jamie didn't respond.

Now she knew. She had never seen a more guilty-looking Jamie.

"Jamie, what did you do? Did you talk to Chris? Did you tell him my dress size?"

"Well, I told you he called a couple times when you weren't here. You already know that he's really nice, Hailey, and we talked a bit. He may have mentioned wanting to get you something. And he may have asked a few questions. And I may have mentioned your size. But I had no idea that he was planning all of this!"

"Jamie! Why didn't you tell me? You didn't even mention that you'd had longer than a ten second conversation with him!"

"I wasn't going to ruin his surprise! If I'd told you we had talked, you would have drilled me on our conversation."

"What else did you talk about?" Hailey demanded, hoping Jamie had revealed nothing more personal about her than her dress size. Then her eyes flew wide as she suddenly put some pieces of the puzzle together. "Jamie, did you tell Chris anything about our rent being due?"

Jamie shrugged. "He said that you'd sounded stressed and discouraged last time he'd talked to you. I think I said that you felt bad about losing your job and might have been worried about the rent."

Hailey glared at Jamie and opened her mouth to give her a stern lecture. How dare she discuss their financial problems with Chris!

Before she could properly explode, Jamie held up her hand to stop the torrent. "Wait! Don't be mad. I didn't do anything wrong. I also told him that you had mentioned getting your check from Grant's. You had assured me that you had it taken care of, so I'd assumed your check had been enough to cover it."

"Did you also happen to mention anything about our landlady?" she asked, her voice deceptively calm.

"Well . . . I may have mentioned that each month was stressful for both of us because Loretta Whipple was not a very understanding person, and we knew that if we ever missed a payment, she would evict us in a heartbeat."

Hailey groaned and rolled her eyes.

"What?" Jamie asked. "It's the truth! I didn't say anything wrong!"

"What's wrong is that Chris charmed our cantankerous landlady and paid our rent for SIX MONTHS!

Jamie visibly paled. "I had no idea!"

"There's no way we can accept all of this!" Hailey anguished, gesturing wildly to include the packages and gifts strewn around the room.

"Well, I'm certainly not going to be the one to take their new things away from them," Jamie said, tilting her head toward the kids. Shaya was carefully inspecting each piece of her art kit, Sylvie was cradling her baby and singing a lullaby, and Spencer had his mom's laptop out and was checking out the baseball academy's website.

"There's no way I'm going to do it!" Hailey shot back.

"Then I think we only have two options," Jamie said. "We pay him back for the rent and all this stuff, or you marry him."

Hailey's mouth dropped open in shock, and she began sputtering. "Jamie, there's no way . . . I can't . . ."

Jamie started laughing. Somewhere in the gales of laughter, Hailey figured out Jamie had just been teasing. But she didn't find it funny at all.

Jamie eventually gained control. "I'm sorry, Hailey, I just couldn't resist. You should have seen the look on your face! Seriously though, the more I think about it, the more it seems like you should just say thank you. It's something he obviously wanted to do. You might run the risk of hurting him if you refuse his gifts and insist on paying the money back. I don't like the idea of him paying and giving so much, but he's obviously done it because he cares about you and us. When someone gives a gift from the heart, even an extravagant one, sometimes the most gracious thing you can do is accept it and say thank you. In this case, you should thank him with both words and one, long, romantic kiss."

Hailey felt herself blushing at the mere thought of kissing Chris.

"Now go try on that gorgeous dress, Hailey! I want to see how it looks!"

Hailey numbly obeyed. It fit perfectly. Hailey had never had such a garment before. In fact, she didn't know that she had ever seen such an exquisite dress. It looked like something a movie star might wear to the Oscars. The neckline was rounded extending in tiny cap sleeves that perched on the edge of her shoulders. The bodice was fitted around her torso and waist, and then gradually flared out into the floor length skirt. It was a beautiful silky, Christmas-red material with delicate gold embroidery beginning in a narrow section on the left side of her waist and then trailing down, cascading out to cover the bottom of the skirt.

As she looked at herself in the mirror, she tried to quell the butterflies in her stomach. She somehow knew that tonight was the night she would find out the true identity of her wonderful, romantic Santa. Maybe Jamie was right. Maybe she should just thank him for blessing her and her family. And maybe she should give him that kiss as well.

CHAPTER 18

Hailey scanned the large room. Chris had to be here somewhere.

He'd called earlier in the day, making sure she was still planning on keeping up her end of the deal. He hadn't talked long though, saying that he was busy with some last minute details at work that had to be done before Christmas. He'd said that if Jamie could drop Hailey off at the party, he would be happy to bring her home. Hailey was fine with that arrangement; it would save her having to deal with finding parking space.

Judging from the number of people crowding the large convention center room, parking would have definitely been a challenge. Grant's had a lot of employees, and this Christmas party was for both them and their families. It was nice to see smiling people of all ages crowding around the special activities around the room. Games, crafts, and other booths lined the perimeter while the center was reserved for the entertainment and tables for people to sit and eat from the huge buffet.

Hailey had been a little worried that she would be overdressed in her red gown, but she saw many of the other guests in formal attire as well. The evening was to end with dancing, and it appeared that many were planning to participate.

Hailey suddenly realized how ridiculous it was for her to be looking for Chris. She had no idea what he looked like! He could be right next to her and she would never know. Just when she decided to give up and wait for him to find her, she saw him.

Near the stage was a large Christmas tree. By the tree was a chair. On the chair was Santa Claus.

Hailey laughed. Even from far away, she knew Chris would be the one dressed in the Santa suit with the long line of kids waiting to sit on his lap. Of course he would. At this rate, he would probably still be dressed in the suit at Easter, and she would never know who he really was.

Hailey saw Chris's eyes light up the moment she came close enough for him to recognize. She winked at him, and then immediately set to work. She took the camera from a very relieved teenager and began taking pictures. The parents wrote their names and email addresses on a list so the pictures could be sent to them.

Eventually, the line was gone; kids had done their Santa visits and moved on to other activities.

Chris stood from the chair and reached for Hailey's hand. Drawing her forward, she felt his beard tickle her ear as he whispered. "And what does Hailey Rhodes want for Christmas?"

Hailey looked into his blue eyes and said seriously, "I want the same thing I've wanted for the past month. Who are you?"

Chris held her gaze for a moment, and Hailey thought she saw a glimmer of fear in their depths. Then, still clutching her hand, he turned and led her across the room to a door hidden behind some decorative foliage.

Hailey followed him out the door, finding herself in the foyer at the back entrance to the convention center. Since everyone had entered through the front of the building, Hailey assumed the line of outside doors at this entrance were probably locked. The overhead lights were dimmed and the area was empty of guests. Chris led her next to the Christmas tree that stood on display, illuminated with soft white lights.

He turned to face her, saying "I'm sorry I wasn't able to talk long earlier today. In fact, I'm sorry I haven't been able to talk much at all the past week. Work has been crazy, and I've been out of town. You mentioned on the phone earlier that you had some good news?"

Hailey had the distinct impression that Chris was stalling, but she figured she'd go along with it for a while.

"I got a job!" she said. "Please thank your sister for delivering my resume. I had an interview yesterday with that private school. The principal called today and offered me the job teaching 2nd grade! I start the day after New Year's!"

"Hailey, that's wonderful! I'm sorry you lost your job as a buyer, but this is good too, right? You liked teaching before?

"I love teaching. I didn't understand why God would let me so unfairly lose my job at Grant's, but now I know He had something even better for me!"

"Don't you love it when you get to see God's plan work out like that? Most times you don't get to see it, but sometimes you do."

Hailey nodded. "I know what you mean. I'm trying to trust God more—with everything. When we first talked on the phone, you reminded me that God had a plan for my life and pretty much said I needed to make my feelings match the reality of what I know about God. Through everything that's happened recently, I guess I've really learned that God can even use bad circumstances for my good."

Hailey paused and looked at Chris thoughtfully. "I don't know who you are, Chris, but I really think you're one of my undeserved blessings from God. Thank you for paying my rent. Thank you for buying my family presents. But most of all, thank you for being the kind of man who would think to do those things. You know I'm very curious, but I really don't care who you are or what you look like. I already know who you are inside."

Chris reached up his hand, and Hailey knew he was going to remove his hat. Her heart beat fast, and she felt a strange, sudden fear. Reaching out, she stopped his hand and held it in hers. Holding his gaze steady with her own, she slowly reached up and removed his hat herself. Dark, wavy hair caught the light from the tree. Hailey stood on her tiptoes, her face mere inches from his. Then closing her eyes, she pulled down the white Santa beard and gently kissed his lips.

Chris wrapped his arms around her and pulled her even closer. If possible, her heart rate accelerated even more as Chris responded, and her sweet, gentle kiss turned into something much deeper. His kiss wasn't demanding at all. It was loving in a way Hailey had never experienced. Hailey didn't know his full name, didn't know what he looked like, and yet she didn't ever want to stop kissing him.

The sound of a door opening startled Hailey and Chris apart.

A man walked toward them, his eyes focused on Chris, apparently clueless that he had interrupted anything. "I've been searching for you, Mr. Wright."

CHAPTER 19

Hailey turned to Chris in shock. Mr. Wright? Had he said Mr. Wright? As in the CEO of Grant's department store? As in the Mr. Wright who had walked in on her and Connor in the break room?

The man continued speaking, oblivious of the bombshell he'd just dropped. "Did you want to speak before the dancing started?"

"Darrel, why don't you go ahead and give the Merry Christmas greeting this year," Chris / Mr. Wright replied. "I wasn't planning on sticking around tonight, so consider yourself in charge from here on out."

"Yes, sir!" Darrel replied. "Have a good evening and a Merry Christmas, sir!"

Darrel went back through the door, closing it behind him and leaving the foyer in silence.

In a frustrated gesture, Chris removed the white Santa beard completely and tossed it to the floor. He turned his breathtakingly handsome features to Hailey, silently begging her to understand.

In yet another almost sickening blow, Hailey recognized his face. She'd seen that same chiseled jaw and masculine features on the cover of Jamie's magazine of the 'Hottest Bachelors in Cincinnati."

Hailey backed away from Chris, her eyes wide with shock. "Mr. Wright? I don't understand. You're Chris, a department store Santa. You're not supposed to be the CEO! And you're also not supposed to be the 'hottest bachelor in Cincinnati!"

Chris grimaced. "Hailey, let me explain."

"Is this some kind of sick joke? Some kind of game to you?"

"No, not all. Please, let me explain." he begged, clearly miserable. "My name is Christian Wright. More specifically, Christian Grant Wright. Grant's was started by my mother's family over a hundred years ago. Though the family still has a few token positions on the board, my position as CEO wasn't handed to me. I had to earn it. Because of my family's wealth and my own success, I get a lot of women who are interested in me romantically. Unfortunately, I always question their motives, unsure if they are more attracted to me or my money. When I met you, I liked you immediately and saw the opportunity for a relationship that wasn't distorted by the usual distractions of who I am. Forgive me, Hailey. It was very selfish. But you didn't know who I was, and I couldn't resist the chance to find out if you could like me for me."

"So this has all been some kind of test?"

Chris paused, considering her question before answering softly. "I guess in a way it was a test. But I can't tell you how happy I am that you passed. From that first night, I thought you were someone special, but, even if I could know that you really cared for me, I knew I would have to jump through a bunch of hoops if we had a shot of being together. It's not as if this month has been easy for me either."

"What do you mean?"

"I had to fire you twice! Like I said, I was selfish. I wanted you for me, but I've always had to be very careful about not having a relationship with someone I work with or another Grant's employee. As CEO, I have to be very careful that there isn't even a hint of questionable behavior. So I arranged for Jerry to fire you so I could date you with a clear conscience. Of course, it was true that we were looking to reduce the workforce in your department, so firing you was very convenient. But then, Jerry sent your resume in for the buyer position, and Connor ended up hiring you. I couldn't say anything without giving away my personal reasons."

"I can't believe you didn't tell me though! You sat through my entire board room presentation as if we had never met and I was the most boring woman on the planet!

"You have no idea how terrified I was that you would recognize me. I thought you'd for sure know my voice."

"I should have! But I was so preoccupied and afraid about getting through my presentation that I really didn't pay much attention to you. Besides, it's hard to recognize something you're not expecting."

Chris shook his head. "You did so well at that presentation! I was so proud of you but so very discouraged as well. I didn't know what to do. Our phone conversations and that night at the Downtown Dazzle had made me even more sure that I wanted you in my life, but I didn't know how that could happen with you still a Grant's employee."

"But then I conveniently provided a marvelous excuse for firing me from that job as well," Hailey filled in.

Christian grimaced. "It wasn't exactly my first choice method, but it served its purpose. "

Hailey felt embarrassed to know that it had been Chris who had walked in on Connor kissing her. She suddenly couldn't look Chris in the eye.

"I can't believe I was so stupid to think that Connor was you," she murmured.

"Don't be too hard on yourself, Hailey," Chris said. Then, frowning, he continued. "I know Connor and I do share a certain family resemblance."

Hailey's eyes flew wide. "You're related?"

"Connor is my cousin. We're both Grants."

Hailey felt instant relief. Maybe she hadn't been so crazy after all. That certainly explained how their voices had sounded alike. They were also both tall, with dark hair and a similar body type.

Chris continued. "Though Connor and I look alike, we've never gotten along. Connor doesn't really have much to do with the Grant side of the family unless he wants something. I earned my job on my own merits. I didn't want it given to me because I was a Grant. Connor, on the other hand, had our grandfather pull some strings to get him hired at Grant's. I've never liked Connor and have pretty much tried to stay clear of him, not wanting my personal feelings to have an influence on his position."

On the heels of Hailey's relief, however, was more embarrassment as she realized how awkward it must have been for Chris to see Hailey with *his cousin*.

Her shame must have shown on her face, for Chris moved forward, closing the space between them.

"I'm so sorry," she said, refusing to meet his eyes. "What you saw in the break room . . ."

Chris gently reached out and nudged Hailey's chin up so she was looking at him once again.

"Don't feel bad about it, Hailey. Yes, I was upset initially, especially because I knew what a player Connor was. I didn't think you were the type of girl to be involved with a guy like him. But then you explained to me what happened. Connor's behavior was inexcusable. By the way, after I found out the truth about what had happened with you, I did a little more digging into Connor Montgomery. I think a lot of his behavior was being overlooked by others because of his family connections. I, however, didn't have a problem firing him."

Chris held up his hand to stop her words. "Now don't feel bad about him being fired. It was very deserved, and it really had nothing to do with you. I should have kept better tabs on him. It's difficult knowing that his inappropriate behavior at Grant's was far more extensive than what you were involved in. Now knowing the extent of Connor's misdeeds, I am embarrassed for myself and my family. Most of my family are Christians, but Connor is not. While that is in no way an excuse for his behavior, it may help explain it. I should also tell you that, after seeing some of the security tapes, I had to have a serious meeting with Andrea Holt as well; the end result being that she, along with Connor, is no longer working for Grant's."

"I still feel bad about it," Hailey admitted. "I should have used better judgment. And knowing what you saw as you walked into that room is more than a little humiliating."

"Look at it this way, Hailey. That experience was what let me fire you, which I really wanted to do. And it let me know that you really did care." Chris's eyes sparkled mischievously. "After all, you only kissed Connor because you thought you were kissing me."

Now Hailey felt her face turn flaming red.

Laughing at her reaction, Chris continued. "After you admitted that, I knew you truly cared for me, so then I was able to pay your rent and give your family gifts like I'd wanted to but without fear that you'd care about me just for the things I could give you. I hope it's okay that I sent them to you before Christmas. I wanted you to have the dress, and I also didn't want you and Jamie stressing if you didn't have enough for the kids."

"It was perfect, Chris," Hailey said softly, marveling that he had been so thoughtful. "But as much as I appreciate it, I can't say I'm completely comfortable with everything you did. Six months' rent is way too much, and I fully intend to pay you back."

Chris gently placed a finger on her lips, silencing her words. "No. It's something I wanted to do. Because I care about you, what concerns you concerns me. I won't accept any reimbursement from you."

"But I still don't understand why you care. You're the CEO of a nation-wide company, and just look at you! I'm sure you could take your 'hottest bachelor' campaign national!"

Chris looked at her seriously. "Hailey, you're everything I could ever want. You're smart and beautiful. You're sweet and caring. I love that you are so gifted with kids. I love that you gave up everything to come help your sister. I love the way you bought that little boy another toy after he broke his that first night. It probably sounds cliché, but I fell for you hard that first night. Then I just had to convince you to go out with a guy dressed in a Santa suit."

"I still can't believe the CEO moonlights as the store Santa."

"I like it. And I like the fact that no one knows me. This year had the added benefit of a certain wager that yielded fantastic dividends."

"You cheated," Hailey said playfully.

"Of course I did," he returned, pulling her closer, and then softly whispering. "There was no way I was going to let you get away."

His lips feathered a gentle kiss on hers. "Please forgive me," he whispered, his eyes meeting hers in a sincere expression of longing. Then, seeming to find something in her face that he was looking for, he kissed her again. This time, his kiss was a long, slow, gentle caress. His fingers tangled in her hair. Hailey's heart rate increased to the point she thought it might burst. And in that moment, all Hailey's anger over Chris's crazy month-long relationship test vanished, and she suddenly saw it all in the light of romance.

As their kiss ended, Chris continued to hold Hailey wrapped in his arms. She laid her head on his shoulder.

"I forgive you," she said softly. "Just please don't fire me from this job!"

Chris smiled and Hailey knew he understood she was referring to her current position in his arms. "Never," he whispered, placing a kiss gently against her forehead. "Why don't we get out of here? I have a company vehicle waiting here at the back entrance. I promise to have you home before midnight . . . or 5 AM at the latest."

Hailey couldn't resist.

After retrieving her coat, she met Chris, who had shed the Santa costume in favor of an elegant suit, and they escaped hand-in-hand out the back entrance. Snow was falling lightly, making the whole word seem quiet, romantic, and peaceful.

Halfway across the parking lot, Hailey abruptly stopped. "Wait a minute, our agreement was that I would be your date for the party. I don't recall your wager including anything other than that."

Hailey saw sudden insecurity flash through Chris's usually confident gaze, and it gave her perverse delight. He had given her such a hard time over the past month that he deserved a little teasing.

Then Hailey's gaze collided with the 'company vehicle' waiting at the end of the parking lot in the softly falling snow. It was a horse drawn carriage, looking as if it was posing for a beautiful Christmas postcard.

"But . . . I definitely wouldn't mind losing another bet to you."

Chris laughed and pulled her into his arms. Holding her close, he whispered in her ear, "How about this? I already know I'm in love with you, Hailey. I know it's only been a month, but every day has made me more sure that you are the woman I've been waiting for. Give me six months. If you just give me six months, I know I can make you fall in love with me too."

"No, I don't think that wager will work," Hailey replied. Then, looking deep in the eyes that had haunted her dreams for the past month, she continued. "Don't you know, Santa? I'm pretty sure you've already won that bet."

Laughing, Chris picked her up, swinging her around in a full circle before setting her back on the ground and thoroughly kissing her.

"Don't you remember, Hailey? Bets I'm sure to win are the only ones I like to make."

As Chris helped her into the carriage, Hailey decided she would like nothing more than to lose many more bets to her Secret Santa.

Other books by Amanda Tru:

YESTERDAY series:
Yesterday
The Locket
Today (Coming Soon)
The Choice (Coming Soon)

TRU EXCEPTIONS series:
Baggage Claim
Mirage
Point of Origin

**Now, please enjoy the following Sneak Peek
of Amanda Tru's
Christian Romantic Suspense series . . .**

Baggage Claim

Chapter 1

"We are having some trouble locating your luggage, Miss Saunders."

"I realize that," Rachel replied dryly. "And that is why I'm here at the Lost Luggage counter."

Rachel's bad attitude and impatience didn't seem to register with the dark-haired attendant as she stared at the computer screen with a furrowed brow.

"You came from Helena, Montana. Had a layover in Cincinnati. But neither of those places has record of your suitcase."

This was taking forever! They had already been over all of this! Did this airline send people who couldn't cut it in other departments to man Lost Luggage? This was ridiculous!

She would say that she had the worst luck ever, but that wasn't necessarily the case. She was, after all, here in New York on an all-expense paid trip that she had won through a nationally syndicated talk show.

Rachel glanced nervously at the clock and the front door of the airport. The shuttle for her hotel was scheduled to leave at any time. If she missed this one, she had no idea when another one would be available.

"Look, Stacy," Rachel said, reading the attendant's name badge and trying to get her attention off her computer and on to Rachel's situation. "I'm in a big hurry. The shuttle for my hotel is leaving right now. Can you just have it delivered to me there when you find it?"

"Oh, yes!" Stacy brightened, as if this was a great idea that had never occurred to her. "What hotel are you staying at?"

"The InterContinental at Times Square."

"Great. Okay, let me just run in back and get a form for you to fill out." She quickly scurried through a door.

Seriously? Rachel wanted to beat her head against the counter. To make matters worse, Stacy was gone an exceptionally long time. After impatiently tapping her foot for five minutes and feeling adrenaline course through her veins, Rachel finally sighed and gave up. She knew she'd missed the shuttle. Now she'd have to hire a taxi to take her to the hotel. That pretty penny would definitely not be included in the "free trip."

To make matters worse, Rachel was not the only one waiting. Four other people, probably also with lost luggage, were in line behind her. They were growing increasingly impatient as well, whispering, shifting their weight back and forth between their feet, and sending accusatory glares in Rachel's direction. Rachel knew that, in their minds, she was at the head of the line, therefore any delay must be her fault.

Unconsciously, Rachel began impatiently drumming her fingers on the counter. How long was this going to take? This was her first time in New York, and she really didn't want to miss any of her group's planned activities.

"Excuse me," Rachel felt an insistent tap on her shoulder and turned around to find a strikingly handsome man in line behind her. Under the Wikipedia definition of 'tall, dark, and handsome,' Rachel was sure she'd find a picture of this man.

"I'm sure you drumming your fingers ad nauseam on a counter is considered highly entertaining for everyone back on the farm, but here in the real world, it is considered highly annoying to anyone with an IQ above 40."

Rachel felt her face warm up. She was embarrassed. She hadn't even realized she had been incessantly drumming her fingers. But, she was also angry. He could have been nice about it, but instead he'd just earned the title of "The-Rudest-Man-Rachel-Had-Ever-Met." In the battle between her embarrassment and anger, anger won.

Pointedly, Rachel looked the man over from his dark, wavy hair to his expensive shoes. "Well, sir, if you are the finest male specimen New York has to offer, I think I'll stick with those 'back on the farm.' I'll have to remember to mark in my travel guide that along with some of the tallest buildings, unsuspecting tourists can also encounter The Rudest Man."

"Sweetheart, if you are naive enough to think me intolerable, then you'd better get right back on a plane and go back to the farm where you belong, with or without your luggage."

Now, Rachel didn't feel she'd gain any points by clarifying that she lived on a ranch, not a farm. How did he even know she was from the country? She hated to think it was that obvious. She'd taken pains to dress stylish, wear her medium blonde hair loose in a current style, and not look as obvious as one of the Beverly Hillbillies.

Rachel opened her mouth to tell the man exactly what she thought of him, but the airline attendant came back through the door with a paper in hand.

"Just fill this out, Miss Saunders, and we'll have your suitcase delivered as soon as possible.

Rachel began filling out the information. She mentally kicked herself for even checking that suitcase. She had wanted to wear something nice to the Broadway show and hadn't wanted to stuff it into a carry-on. But right now, rumpled clothes would be far better than none at all! Stacy went back to her computer, showing no inclination to help the other people in line.

"Excuse me," The Rudest Man said to the attendant. "Do you think you could help someone else while she's filling that out?

"I'm sorry, sir," the Stacy replied. "Let me finish with her, then I'll help whoever is next."

There were obvious groans and snorts of indignation from the others in line. As terrible as it was, Rachel felt a surge of pleasure that the jerk was going to have to wait a little longer.

Finishing, Rachel handed the form back to Stacy. "I'm only in New York for the weekend. Exactly how long is it going to take to locate my suitcase?"

"I'm not sure," Stacy replied, her brow furrowed once again. "I have another guy on a computer back there trying to locate it. Let me just run back real quick and ask him what he thinks."

"No, no!" Rachel tried to protest. The rest of the people in line would probably just lynch her right there if, because of her, the attendant disappeared indefinitely a second time. "You don't need to . . ."

As Stacy started through the door, a man came through holding something black in his arms.

"That's my suitcase!" Rachel squealed.

The man, unsmiling, came around the counter, plopped the suitcase down beside Rachel and disappeared back the way he came.

"Thank you, George!" Stacy said, beaming at what she probably felt was her own success in locating the missing luggage.

Graciously overlooking the drama and thanking Stacy for her help, Rachel pulled out the handle to wheel the suitcase to the door.

"Maybe you should look inside to make sure everything is there," The Rudest Man offered. "You don't want any surprises."

Stacy bristled. "No one at this airline would ever open a suitcase without serious cause or permission. It's strictly against policy."

"I'm sure it is," The Rudest Man replied. "Nevertheless . . ."

"This is my suitcase. I'm sure it's fine." Rachel said, addressing Stacy and completely ignoring the man. She was not about to follow any advice from him, if just for the sake of principle. "I'm in a big hurry. I'll look it over when I get to the hotel. If there's anything wrong, trust me, I won't be shy about it."

Hurrying away before she received any more unwanted comments or advice, Rachel went through the sliding doors. She was relieved to see several classic New York yellow taxis parked at a curb. This country girl had never even ridden in a taxi before. Hopefully there weren't some kind of unwritten protocol or rules about hiring a taxi that she didn't know about. Her education on taxis and New York in general consisted of what she had learned from TV shows.

As she walked toward the cars, one of the cabbies jumped out.

"Here, Miss," he said. "I'll stick that suitcase in the trunk for you and then you can tell me where you're headed.

Relieved, Rachel slid into the back seat, told the driver the name of her hotel, and prayed the ride wouldn't cost all of her spending money.

She had been so excited to be one of four lucky winners to win the contest and get to go to New York to see a filming of the sponsoring talk show, a Broadway production, and other tourist destinations. She had always had notoriously bad luck and hadn't won a single contest in her life. Yet, when she had actually won this free trip, she thought her luck had changed. But, after being randomly selected twice by security for full body screenings that seemed to include everything but a blood test, she had been seated on the airplane between two very large men, at least one of which spent the flight passing some very unfortunate and possibly toxic gas. Follow that up with lost luggage and a missed hotel shuttle, and suddenly her luck wasn't looking so good.

Thankfully, other than a few pleasantries, the cabbie wasn't overly talkative. Rachel was glued to the window, feeling very much like a country hick in the city for the first time. She did appreciate the few times the cabbie pointed out interesting landmarks. The ride took longer than Rachel expected, and, when the cab finally pulled up in front of the impressive InterContinental Times Square Hotel, she tried to appear very calm and collected as she handed the cabbie his wad of cash. How could people in New York afford to regularly hire taxis?

Rachel got out of the car, and the cabbie popped the trunk for her to get her suitcase. She lifted it out and stepped to the curb as the cab pulled away.

"Rachel!"

Surprised, Rachel looked up from battling to get her suitcase set on its wheels. Before she could even move, a dark-haired man ran up, grabbed her close, and kissed her passionately on the mouth. Rachel went completely numb, too shocked to even think. He finally pulled away, continuing to hold her close and grin at her like she was the absolute best thing in his life.

"Sweetheart! I'm so glad you're here!" he said joyfully.

Recognition hit. This wasn't a complete stranger. She knew this man! He was 'The Rudest Man' from the airport, only now, he obviously wasn't acting so disagreeable. Indignation rose in her. How dare he! Her hand itched to slap him full in the face. As if he realized her intention, he blocked her hand and held it firmly in his continued embrace.

Bending close and smiling, he whispered in her ear. "I'm an agent with Homeland Security. If you want both of us to survive the next ten seconds, you'll play along and do exactly as I say."

Rachel's brain was too shocked to put together any reasoning or coherent thought. Fortunately, her body seemed to take over, switching to a highly competent autopilot.

As the agent released his vise-like grip on her hands, Rachel smiled, reached up, and wrapped her arms around his neck. If her life depended on her playing this part, then she was going to aim for an Oscar.

Rachel was tall, but she had to stand on her tiptoes as she snuggled closer and kissed him lightly. Responding, he kissed her back, his fingers tangling in her long, wavy hair and his lips seeming to thoroughly savor hers.

Rachel was lucid enough to realize this agent was very accomplished in the art of kissing. She was left breathless and with heart palpitations, which of course she attributed entirely to the danger they were in.

"I'm taking you to dinner right now," the agent said, taking her suitcase in one hand and holding her hand in the other. "You can check into your hotel later."

He quickly urged her into a waiting taxi, sliding in beside her with her suitcase on his lap.

As he shut the door, the driver immediate pulled out and began weaving through traffic.

"We're being followed," the man said. "Sit close and act like we're still enjoying each other."

"Who is following us?" Rachel asked, fighting the urge to turn around and try to spot the enemy. She obediently scooted closer to him and inclined her head towards his.

Instead of answering her question, the agent wasted no time in propping the suitcase on his lap and unzipping it.

"What are you doing?" Rachel demanded. Still, the agent didn't answer

"That's my suitcase!" Even Rachel realized that she was starting to shriek. "Who are you? Would someone please tell me what's going on!"

"My name is Dawson Tate," the man replied simply and calmly as he lifted the lid on the suitcase.

Dawson reached in and moved aside a few of Rachel's clothes and undergarments. Rachel's protests died on her lips. Beneath the top layer of clothes was nestled a complicated looking contraption. The only part she could identify was what looked to be a blank display, like on a digital clock.

Shocked, Rachel stammered, "Is that a . . . a .....?"

Understanding her unfinished question, Dawson answered calmly, "Yes, it's a bomb."

BAGGAGE CLAIM may be purchased from the same online store where you purchased this book.

Thanks for reading!

You can find Amanda Tru at her blog or on Facebook!

http://amandatru.blogspot.com

http://www.facebook.com/amandatru.author